Self-Portrait with Ghosts

KELLY DWYER

SCEPTRE

Copyright © 1999

First published in 1999 by Hodder and Stoughton
A division of Hodder Headline PLC
A Sceptre book

The right of Kelly Dwyer to be identified as the Author of
the Work has been asserted by her in accordance with the
Copyright, Designs and Patents Act 1988.

10 9 8 7 6 5 4 3 2 1

British Library C.I.P.
A CIP catalogue record for this title
is available from the British Library.

ISBN 0 340 73947 9

Printed and bound in Great Britain by
Mackays of Chatham PLC, Chatham, Kent

Hodder and Stoughton
A division of Hodder Headline PLC
338 Euston Road
London NW1 3BH

I am very grateful to the Wisconsin Arts Board for a generous grant.

I thank my father, Richard Dwyer, and my in-laws, Rita and Lou Venclovas, for providing me with home, food, moral support, and other necessities, and luxuries, while I concentrated on my writing. In the hard times, their gracious generosity made it possible.

To my brother, Dean Dwyer, my cousin Michael Dwyer, and my sisters-in-law Audra Wenzlow and Victoria Siliūnas: Thanks for your loving and biased enthusiastic encouragement. I'm additionally indebted to Viki for creating the ceramics that inspired Kate's, and for answering my questions about her craft. I thank my brother-in-law Rimas Siliūnas for investing in this novel in countless ways, including laptop and Bambino's runs; and my nieces, Andreja and Amelija, who energized and delighted me with their joyful antics, even as they interrupted my writing. To the "Mademoiselles Dwer," Caitlin and Brenan: Thanks for being yourselves.

I'm immeasurably grateful to my editor, Faith Sale, for being the best reader I could have—wise, insightful, and caring—for asking just the right questions at the right time, and for always believing I could do more. My agent Henry Dunow's guidance, encouragement, and support have been invaluable. I also thank Laura Gaines Jofre for helping me through early revisions, Anna Jardine for her copyediting, and Aimée Taub for her dedication.

And finally, I thank Louis Wenzlow, for putting so much of his mind and soul into every page of this book, and for making such good coffee.

To the men
LOUIS AND DAD

Something we were withholding made us weak,
Until we found out that it was ourselves.
  —ROBERT FROST, "The Gift Outright"

"Would you tell me, please, which way I ought to go from here?"

"That depends a good deal on where you want to get to," said the Cat.

"I don't much care where—" said Alice.

"Then it doesn't matter which way you go," said the Cat.

"—so long as I get somewhere," Alice added as an explanation.

"Oh, you're sure to do that," said the Cat, "if you only walk long enough."

  —LEWIS CARROLL, *Alice's Adventures in Wonderland*

Self-Portrait with Ghosts

Interrupted

The sky is the wrong color for this. It should be a sick yellow-ish green, tornado-weather color, not this vibrant, pellucid blue, this bright wash of unreflected light. The palm trees and shrubs shaped like Mickey, Pluto, and Dumbo are wrong as well; there should be pine trees, twisted birches, deadly hemlocks, a forest in a European fairy tale hiding danger, wolves, a man in a cloak. It's the man in the cloak she's worried about now, or rather, his Disneyland twin with the cowboy boots and jeans, the one who was standing a few feet away from Kate and Audrey while they were waiting in line for ice cream. "Why, your daughter sure is a cute one," he said. "Just about as pretty as her mom." Kate was annoyed, thinking this was just a stupid pick-up line, but now she understands that he said this only to fluster her. To distract her.

The important thing, she tells herself, is not to panic. It would only cloud her mind, and she needs to think clearly. "Have you seen my daughter, my little girl? The little girl who was standing right behind me?" she asks the other people in line. They shake their heads, all but one, a kindly-looking elderly woman, who says, "I saw her," and Kate feels so grateful, so relieved, she is close to laughter when she asks, "Where?" The woman smiles, points to a nearby bench. Kate searches for the familiar auburn hair and freckled nose of her young daughter, but she sees only an adolescent girl with pasty white skin and budding breasts, chewing on a rope of black licorice. Her knees are dirty, her pink T-shirt too tight; it sticks to her skin, stretching under the arms. Audrey looks nothing like this girl—would never wear a shirt that wasn't a size too big, would never wear pink, a color for Barbies and poodles, wouldn't eat black licorice if it were the last junk food on this earth—but for a moment Kate finds herself squinting, tilting her head, trying to get this stranger to look like, to become, her daughter.

Kate is clutching the Drumsticks too hard: the ice cream tops fall to the tidy cobblestone ground; the waffle bottoms squash between her fingers, and she shakes them off. Her hands are sticky and wet, but this is meaningless, and she uses them to wipe the hair from her face. Slowly she turns around, examining every inch of Adventureland with her laser-keen eyes. When she is back where she began, between the ice cream cart and the bench, facing the Pirates of the Caribbean, she glimpses a blue uniform and a glittering badge. She runs to the security guard.

"I can't find my daughter," she says, and the man nods, sympathetic and patient—I have seen this a thousand times, he is saying with his eyes—and tells her to calm down.

"You want me to calm down? I told you, my daughter is gone. She may have been kidnapped."

"I'm sure she'll turn up, now—"

Kate begins to shout. Her words may or may not be comprehensible to others; she herself has little idea what she is saying. Something about calling the police, a man in cowboy boots, suing Disneyland's kitschy, capitalistic ass: she is like a drunk person standing on a street corner shouting about a conspiracy, a murder suspect loudly insisting upon her innocence, a wild-eyed woman unsteadily wielding a gun while proclaiming nobody's gonna get hurt. In some part of her is the realization, *So this is what it means to be out of your mind with fear.* The security guard is telling her to get ahold of herself, but Kate cannot help it. She shouts louder and louder. And louder.

Kate awakened to the sound of her own mumbled voice, and checked the clock beside her bed: six-fifteen. Practically the middle of the night, but she knew that she couldn't possibly fall back to sleep. She pulled on a pair of sweats and cotton sport socks, quietly walked down the hall, and opened the door to Audrey's room. Her suddenly teenaged daughter (how had she gotten so tall? so old?) was clutching her ancient stuffed polar bear, her eyelids pulsing in some sweet, innocuous dream: about horses, perhaps, or a dewy-faced boy at school. But what did Kate know? She was only her mother, and thus naturally adept at wishful thinking.

Kate studied Audrey's messy auburn hair and freckled, leonine nose. Despite everything, despite her father, she was a normal kid, safe, kind, unaware of danger and betrayal and lies. It seemed a miracle sometimes.

Kate closed the door and went downstairs, into the kitchen.

She ground some French-roast beans, put them into the coffee-maker, and poured in Sparkletts water, which dribbled down the side and onto the counter below. Her hands were trembling slightly. She was about to open the refrigerator door for some juice when she noticed and reread the line of magnetic poetry Audrey had created the week before:

my silver tongue
slides into
your fire engine
and laps
yes yes
rose blue

Kate ran her fingers through her hair and held her hands still at the back of her head. Every time she read these words, she asked herself the same question: What did her barely pubescent daughter know about tongues that slid into fire engines and then lapped yes yes rose blue? Nothing, Kate told herself. Audrey had been trying to shock her, that was all. She had just been reading too much Kerouac and watching too much MTV and listening too much to her best friend, Sandira, who described everything from biceps to bookbags as "sexy." Audrey didn't really know anything about silver tongues and fire engines.

Did she?

Fear. Kate had been filled with it ever since Audrey had turned thirteen, started her period, begun high school—fear of everything from sex and drugs to eating disorders; fear that Audrey would become like one of those teenagers at the mall straggling behind their bewildered mothers on a back-to-school shopping expedition, cynical and sullen, her hipbones jutting from her jeans, her fresh, innocent face bored and pierced all over, like a fish that's been hooked a dozen times; fear that Audrey would simply become her own person so thoroughly that Kate would no longer recognize her—and she was filled with it now, as she sat in her ceramics studio (brightly lit, colorful, anomalously cheery), sipping her coffee, staring at her latest project, at the clay image of her own face.

There was her straight Gaelic nose, her wide, thin-lipped mouth, her squarish jaw, the two sunken mounds of her not-yet-molded eyes. *Your daughter's going to leave you,* she thought, imagining Audrey emerging from the gash in the upper left of her skull. In four years she would be gone, and Kate would be nothing more than the overprotective mother who called her dorm room too often.

Which had come first, Kate wondered, her logical and illogical fears, the nightmares in which she turned around to find Audrey gone, lost, stolen, disappeared, or this unfinished face, this sculpture based on the Birth of Athena, this piece about letting go, about embracing the process of her daughter's growing up? Kate did embrace the process, she did. It was just that there were times when she wished she could have locked Audrey up in the second story of their condo, shaved off her long hair (you couldn't be too cautious), brought her books to read (harmless but edifying, Charles Dickens, Louisa May Alcott, Edna

St. Vincent Millay) and computer games to play (nonviolent ones, naturally), until she was thirty or so. Kate ran her fingers over the gash from which Audrey would emerge, knowing that locking her daughter away would be useless. She would find a way to escape. Everyone did.

"Mom?"

Audrey was standing in the doorway between the studio and the kitchen, wearing running shorts and a tank top for cross-country practice, spooning some blue yogurt concoction into her mouth.

"Hey, good morning."

"I went to wake you, but you weren't there."

"I had the most terrible dream," Kate said, following her into the kitchen. "I dreamed that you were lost at Disneyland, and—"

"Mom, quit dreaming about me."

Audrey was looking at Kate as though her mother had read her journal, eavesdropped on her most private telephone call, rifled through her dresser drawers.

"I'm sorry," Kate said, "I promise I'll never do it again." She shook her head. "Honey, how can I help what I dream about?"

"I don't know, but just don't. It gives me the creeps."

Kate poured herself a second cup of coffee. When she turned around, she saw that Audrey was sitting at the kitchen table, her head half hidden behind a Spanish textbook. Audrey tucked her hair behind her ears—her hands were delicate and soft, her ears fragile mollusks—and reached for her glass, which almost slipped out of her hands. Be careful, Kate wanted to shout, but stopped herself. Audrey would only have given her that look that meant Kate was a crazy person, who needed to be handled with kid gloves. Careful of what? she would have asked politely. Everything, Kate would have replied.

Kate was putting away the clean glasses and plates from the dishwasher when she remembered it was Friday. Her stomach dropped a notch. Friday meant one thing to Kate: her mother. The thought induced in her a multicolored web of emotions: the irritating silvery-gray terbium of a TV on the fritz, the dark anger of a reddish black that could swallow you if you let it, the brilliant green of emeralds, Irish grass, her mother's own sharply focused eyes. If Audrey thought she had it bad, she should try having her sweet, doting, beloved grandmother for a critical, annoying, beloved mother.

"Remember," Kate said, "it's Friday."

Audrey rolled her eyes—speckled, light brown, cat's eyes. "News flash, Mom, I know."

"Why don't I come watch the meet today, and then we can go straight to Grandma's?"

"Coach Bryant's supposed to take us out for pizza after the race. I might go, or I might not. I'll call you if I need a ride."

Kate knew better than to press the issue. If she pretended she didn't care, maybe Audrey would decide to come to her mom's. If Kate told her, "You know, honey, I'd really like it if you ate dinner with us tonight," Audrey might go out for pizza just to spite her, and then Kate would have to deal with the disapproval of her mother, who tended to take any absence at her Friday dinners as a personal insult. After years of serving frozen pizzas, gourmet TV dinners, and Chinese takeout, her mother prepared elaborate meals every Friday night now that Kate was an adult—whether to atone for her earlier sin or because she truly enjoyed cooking once a week, Kate wasn't sure. Her black-bean-and-chèvre enchiladas of two weeks before had been a big hit, but last week Audrey had refused the tournedos with porcini mushroom sauce ("Beef wrapped in bacon strips? I'll never run again"), and Kate knew that if she told her mother Audrey was going out for pizza after her race, she would suspect it was simply a ruse designed to avoid eating the food she had so lovingly prepared.

"Okay," Kate said, making her voice neutral and calm. "Just let me know."

A car honked, and Audrey was out of her seat, out of the kitchen—"Bye Mom see you later!" "Wait! Do you have your lunch? Have a good race!"—and out of the condo, slamming the door, in the time it would have taken Kate to ask herself where she'd left her keys. Gone with the wind, Kate thought, staring at the yogurt congealing on the counter.

What kind of wind? Audrey would ask, sharing her uncle Luke's distaste for clichés. A refreshing ocean breeze, a terrifying twister?

Both, Kate would say. Both.

Kate touched the leather-hard clay face and felt a hum of excitement. The fear was gone now—or rather, swallowed into the back of her mind, nothing more than a useful tool to help her with the sculpture. She loved this moment, when a figure was shaped but not completed, when she could still envision it as perfect, its expression evoking the exact combination of emotions she'd imagined, when reality with its inevitable disappointments was still a few hours away. (You could never render the exact combination; you could never perfectly achieve your vision; the clay had its own mindless vision, too.) She ran her fingers over the ridge of her clay brows and pushed the imperfect future from her mind. She summoned her concentration, saw the finished eyes staring back at her as she wanted them to look—there, that was it, just like that—and then picked up her dowel and dug in.

She had been working for twenty minutes or an hour or maybe even half the morning when the telephone rang. Instead of irritation, she experienced something akin to relief. Her eyes were tired; she could use a break. She reached for the cordless phone.

"Hello?"

"Are you up?" came her mother's gruff voice.

"Of course I'm up."

"Well, I know how you sometimes go back to bed after Audrey leaves for school."

Kate had done this four, maybe five, times in all the years of Audrey's formal education, but her mother, having caught her once, was never going to let her forget it. "I'm not in bed, Mom, I'm in my studio. What's up?"

"I was just checking with you about tonight. I thought I'd make Thai, with that curry dish you and Audrey like so much, and pad thai with extra peanut sauce for Luke. I hope he's feeling okay," she added. "He sounded kind of funny the other night."

"Funny how?"

"I don't know. Just . . . funny."

For as long as Kate could remember, her mother had complained to her about Luke, just as—Kate knew—she complained to him about her, and complained about Colleen to anyone who would listen. Her children were failures, their mother believed, and she had no one to blame but herself, and her husband, who had gone and died on her when she was only thirty-three, leaving her alone with three young kids. "If only your father were alive . . ." Kate had heard variations on this refrain throughout her life. "If only my Grady were here . . ." Then everything would be different, and not just different, of course, but better. Colleen wouldn't exhibit such an uncanny biblical likeness to the Whore of Babylon. Kate wouldn't be hiding away in that gated condominium complex as though it were some females-only menstrual hut. And Luke, Luke would have an ordinary, happy existence, with a wife, or at least a girlfriend, and a car that didn't lurch every time you drove it over fifty. He'd have a job worthy of his talents—as a journalist, or a college professor, maybe even the dean—instead of wasting his brain and education all these years in that bookstore that smelled like cat litter and musty old paperbacks.

"I'm sure he's fine, Mom," Kate said. "You worry about him too much."

"Mothers worry. It's part of the job description, as you well know. Page seven thousand and something, I think it is. I suppose Alek's coming tonight?"

Kate pulled the phone a few inches from her ear and sipped her coffee. Was this how Audrey felt? Did the same catarrhal tremor of irritation that was creeping up her own throat creep up her daughter's when Kate said the equivalent of "I suppose Alek's coming tonight"? Her mother knew very well that Alek was coming tonight—he came with Kate to her mother's every Friday—but had to act as though she didn't care one way or the other whether he came to dinner, whether Kate married him, whether he became a stepfather to Audrey. It was the same tone, Kate imagined, her mother would use at a business meeting, a poker-blank look on her face, when she'd say, "I don't know, the price seems a bit high," about some investment she had every intention of grabbing.

"Yes, Alek's coming," Kate said.

"I'd better make something with shrimp in it, then."

"Mom, don't go to any—"

"Listen, the day it's trouble to make a meal for my family is the day you might as well hammer the last nail into the coffin. Well, I'd love to sit here and gab all day but I'm already late for an appointment. See you tonight."

Kate heard a click, followed by silence, and had to repress the urge to run to her garbage can of clay and punch into it with her fists. If Alek were here, he would laugh at her, asking her what Mommie Dearest had done this time. "Your mom's such a sweetie," he always said. Naturally he said this: he had an endearing, infuriating knack for concentrating on people's good qualities, not their flaws; and besides, he and her mother were allies, of a sort. Kate was stubborn, they agreed. Beneath her tough exterior (just a show, of course) she was really very vulnerable, sensitive, almost tender, still on a decade-long rebound that was clouding her better judgment. She wouldn't know a good thing (Alek Perez, high school history teacher, warm, funny, smart, handsome, great with Audrey, owner of the cutest beach bungalow anyone had ever seen) if it hit her over the head with a sledgehammer.

"Mom's upset because I won't marry you," Kate had told him one day the past summer.

Alek had smiled. He had a beautiful smile, genuinely pleased, open, and sincere, his dark brown eyes smiling along with his mouth; it had been one of the features that had attracted Kate to him in the first place, because anyone who smiled like that, she'd believed, had to be incapable of hiding anything: love, boredom, a secret life, matchbooks inscribed with the names of unfamiliar restaurants.

"Your mother's a wise woman," he'd said. "Call her up, apologize. Tell her the wedding's on."

"And complicate my perfectly wonderful life?"

"Tell me. Wouldn't marrying the right man—if he happened to come along—make your life even more perfect and wonderful?"

"When I see someone with the words 'The Right Man' scrawled on his forehead, I'll let you know."

"You're breaking my heart," Alek said.

Kate's husband had loved her too little, while Alek's wife had loved him too much. Now they seemed destined to live out mild versions of their former spouses' neuroses. With Alek, it had begun quite simply: he had met Violeta in his credit union. She was the dark-haired customer service representative with eyes worthy of her name, and he'd soon found that they shared an interest in cooking, a passion for basketball, and a love of the outdoors.

"Wait a minute," Kate said, when she first heard the story. "You discovered all that when you applied for a loan?"

"Maybe not right then, but soon after. And I was just opening an account."

"Okay, go on," Kate told him. They'd been seeing each other for only a couple of weeks, but already they'd found their common obsessions: holy matrimony, wrongs done to and by, contracts made and broken.

"Violeta was everything I thought I wanted at twenty-six. Loyal, ready for commitment, affectionate . . . maybe too affectionate. Her one flaw, if you could call it that, was that she was a little clingy."

"Clingy?" Kate asked.

"Yeah, you know. She liked to talk on the phone a few times a day, even if we were going to see each other after work, and she was always holding on to me in public, wrapping her arms around my waist and digging her fingers into my ribs. But if anything, I found her devotion flattering. Besides, I was bewitched by her. Six months after we met, we were joined in holy matrimony—forever, I thought at the time."

"A church wedding?" Kate interrupted. She wanted to picture it right.

"Tijuana."

"Tijuana! Oh, Alek. Then what?"

"Within a couple of months, it became clear to me that Violeta's affection was turning into . . . well, some kind of a disease. Her love began to suffocate me, like a blanket over my face I could never remove."

Kate mock-shuddered. "What do you mean?"

"For example. During basketball season, she'd come to the gym every single day after work and watch the team practice. These weren't games, although she went to those too, this was just practice. Or she'd spend half of her paychecks on fancy lingerie, and if I didn't notice, she'd lock herself in the bathroom and sob that I was losing my passion for her. I tell you, I had to memorize every little nightie and bra she had, because if I said, 'Is that new?' and it wasn't, it was just as bad. One time, after I told her I was too tired to have sex, she slept in the bathtub all night."

"No."

"When she started throwing things at me if I came home even ten minutes later than I said I would—"

"Oh, my."

"—I suggested that we see a marriage counselor. She

refused. Then one day she quit her job at the credit union and began to devote her entire days to cooking me dinner. I'd leave for school in the morning, and she'd already be kneading dough. I told her, 'Violeta, the problems in our marriage have nothing to do with your culinary skills. You don't need to do this. Really.' But she was determined. Like she thought that if only she cooked the perfect meal, everything would be fine."

Kate was both delighted and repulsed by Violeta's obsession. She imagined the poor woman must have been devastated when Alek asked for a divorce, but the story didn't end as she had expected.

"I was racked with guilt," Alek said, "and completely terrified of her reaction. I thought she might try to kill herself, or me. Finally I got up the nerve to say I was sorry, but I saw no alternative, I really thought we should get a divorce. I was prepared for anything. Sobbing, screaming, suicide threats, a steak knife at my throat . . . Instead, she said she was relieved."

"Relieved?" Kate repeated.

"Relieved. And tired. Tired of all that expended energy, tired of trying to convince herself that she loved me more than she did, that I was really worthy of her passion, and furthermore—that was her word—furthermore, she had never liked camping."

Alek might have become cynical after that, might have jettisoned his dreams of domestic bliss for a life of frozen pizzas and safe sex with women who were really just friends, might have become the sort of person who says, jokingly, of course, "Marriage is an institution, all right—an institution for the mentally ill." Kate noticed, however, that he talked about his marriage with bemusement, as if to say, through his tone and quizzical expression, Isn't life strange? Isn't love a mystery? and Wasn't I dumb? Yes, dumb. For Alek had learned a lesson from Violeta. In hindsight, he understood that he had fallen in love with her so quickly, so easily, because he'd been seduced by her adoration for him, a mistake, he said wryly, he would never make again. Love, he had come to believe, was not a two-way street, it was two one-way streets that ran parallel to each other, and in the same direction if you were lucky.

"People think they want unconditional love from their mates," Alek had told Kate once, "but it isn't true. We want to have to earn it. To work for it a bit. And we ought to love—how's this for a radical notion?—someone who deserves it."

"Too radical," Kate said.

"Yes, someone with the strange combination of qualities we happen to value. Humor, kindness, a gleaming intelligence in her eyes. The confident way she walks across a room. A stubborn hardheadedness that lets you know this isn't a dress rehearsal but the real thing, and if you screw up you might not get a second chance."

Alek had given her this list in a tone of quiet intensity that had let her know, if she'd been too modest to recognize herself in the description (and at first, she hadn't been at all sure—did she really walk across a room with confidence?), that he was talking about his feelings for her. Kate had been quick to undermine his ardent profession, to put it into perspective with some kind of joke ("Well, anybody would be in love with that person," she'd said), beginning the teasing on the subject that would become their routine. She hadn't been ready to fall into his arms and be told that she was loved; she certainly hadn't been ready to tell him that she loved him, too. And even now, more than two years later, while Kate was very, very fond of Alek, she couldn't quite say that she was in love. Sometimes, staring at his face—his smooth skin the color of walnuts, his dark crescent eyes, the mole to the left of his somewhat flat nose and his high, Mayan cheekbones—or listening to him talk passionately about some great book he'd read or some politician he opposed, or observing his ease in bantering with Audrey, she would feel a tightness in her chest that she knew was an affection and trust she hadn't experienced in years, maybe ever.

But as for love, it was just like Alek to try to theorize about something so inexplicable as if it were Don Cristóbal Aguilar's nineteenth-century struggle over the Los Angeles water supply, a historical fact that could be put into perspective, learned from, and understood. And it was just like him to make love sound rosier than it really was, to smooth over the jagged edges of something that was sharper, deeper, darker, and crazier than anything anyone could say about it, to make it sound all soft lips, wet tongue, and no teeth. When Kate's turn came to talk, to rant and rave about everything from her ex-husband's betrayal to his infuriating habit of putting empty ice cube trays into the freezer, she would tell Alek that his historian's faith in the power of explanations was ill suited when it came to love. What did humor, kindness, and a gleaming intelligence in the eyes have to do with why we loved someone? Women fell for assholes all the time—not because these rakes and cads embodied the virtues otherwise sensible women valued but because of their boyish grins, or their faraway eyes, or because they dared to run their fingers up your leg under a white linen tablecloth. And it wasn't just in made-for-TV movies that men left their wives—women with whom they were perfectly compatible and who had mothered all their dear children—for their not-as-kind secretaries, their not-as-smart co-workers, the middle-aged divorcée who said inappropriate things when she got drunk but who had a low throaty laugh they believed they could not live without, women they didn't respect, admire, or even like all that much, but whom they loved enough to break up everything.

Kate knew all about that. About falling for someone dangerous and exciting (or at least someone who seemed dangerous and exciting because he rode a motorcycle and worked on sports cars instead of going to college, and because he had a voice that made her think of a gravel road shaded by pines, rough and cool at the same time, a voice that could take her someplace she'd never been and from where she might never return), and about being the one left behind. Sam had ended their happy little family life the way other people swatted flies: offhandedly, irrevocably, apparently giving no thought to the feelings of his bothersome victims. He'd had help, of course.

Colleen had always been a troublemaker. Even when they were kids, she was the one who talked to strangers, ate popcorn kernels off the ground, went behind the bushes at the park with scruffy neighborhood boys, yelled bloody murder whenever their mother told her no. But she was also the affectionate one, the one who saved her allowance all year to buy perfect Christmas presents, the one who liked to cuddle and snuggle, the one who never forgot to say her prayers at night, asking God to bless her mommy, her sister, her brother, her daddy in heaven, ending with "I love you, Jesus. Amen." As an adolescent, she became wild, a caged animal let into the Serengeti, bent on going to hell. She swore at their mother, slammed the door behind herself, yelling she'd never return, and then came home hours later, her cheeks flushed and tear-streaked, begging forgiveness, crying into their mother's arms, saying she wanted to wake up and find herself a different person. In high school, it was Colleen who smoked pot, sneaked into bars, drove around town a year before she could even get her learner's permit, came home at four in the morning drunk out of her skull and wearing only one shoe.

Late at night, while they were lying in their matching Scandinavian-style twin beds, Colleen would confess her latest exploits, and Kate would listen to her younger sister, entranced, appalled, and exasperated, and then the next day would cover for her, vowing, always vowing, that this would be the last time—the last time she told their mom Colleen had the flu when she was really drained and immobile at eight A.M. from having done too much coke the night before; the last time she said that Colleen was sleeping over at a friend's after Colleen had called Kate, on their private line, to say that she had gone to a party with a soccer player named Paulo or a jazz musician named Hop, but that the party had turned out to be in Ensenada, or in Santa Cruz, and she didn't think she'd be home before noon; the last time she assured their mother that Colleen truly had studied for the bio exam, the geometry quiz, the Spanish final, when in fact Colleen had been out to a club in L.A., a swim party in the San Pablo Hills, a retirement bash at the Elks Lodge she had crashed, just for fun, on a whim.

Colleen was fucked up, that was for sure, the kind of girl a man ought not to love, if he knew what was good for him, but apparently men did not know, or if they did, they didn't care. Like cigarette smoking, falling in love with Colleen seemed to be unhealthy and painfully addictive. They called at odd hours, day and night; sent flowers that Colleen handed to her mother, shyly, ceremoniously, as if she'd ordered them herself; and some-times came to the house, broodingly handsome guys, pale and lovesick, whom Colleen toyed with the way a cat bats around a mouse, until she got bored and sent them home. Maybe it was this restlessness that made men fall for Colleen. Or maybe it was her charged, focused stare, how she would look a man in the eye and tell him, through her momentarily charmed gaze, You. You're the one. Or perhaps they were attracted to her because they could see that underneath her bravado, her sexual energy, her aura of danger that let them know love was risky and sex was never safe, she was just a nice Catholic girl, a little wild, mixed up, but with a good heart, a sense of penance, and a joie de vivre that must have made God in heaven look down at her with pride: his finest, most irresistible piece of work.

"Where have you gone?" Kate had cried, in a dream

she'd once had, years before. Colleen was hiding somewhere nearby—Kate could hear an occasional giggle—but the night was foggy and pitch-black, and even though Kate groped with her arms stretched out before her, she never found Colleen. Maybe that was what Kate could never get over, never forgive— not that Colleen had stolen her husband, but that she had left her, abandoned her, to a world without a sister, her sister, Colleen. It felt as though she had died, but not died, as though she were no longer alive, but hovering over her, reminding her, always reminding her, of what she'd lost. I've got to tell Colleen about this, Kate must have thought a hundred times in the past decade, beginning to reach for the phone, and then felt a wash of loneliness that was like realizing she was the only one to survive the fire, the flood, the nuclear war. How could she explain this to anyone? She was my sister! she could say, and everyone would nod in understanding, but who could truly understand? Not Alek, who was only a man, or Luke, who was only a brother; not her mom, who had been a self-sufficient only child; or Keisha, her sole woman friend, who wasn't even really a friend but a business associate, an acquaintance, and who had never been close to her siblings. No, Kate knew, the only person who could understand how she felt was Colleen. You were my sister! Kate could say, and Colleen would look into her eyes and then look away. I know, she would say, I know.

Kate picked up a wooden thumb, glanced into the small upright mirror, and began to form the curving ball of her left eye. Her conversation with her mother was in the distant past; all that existed was this moment, her fingers, her tool, her eyes, this clay. The excruciating pain of giving birth out of her head. Had she eaten up Sam, the way Zeus had swallowed Athena's mother, Metis, after having turned her into a fly? Kate supposed she had absorbed him, in a way, but that was a long time ago, and it made no difference now. The important thing was that she was alone, experiencing pain, love, fear—above all, fear—while Audrey was burrowing out of her skull, a teenage goddess of wisdom and war, wearing running shoes, brandishing a sword.

Kate examined this earthly image of herself, this face that looked like hers but was not, not exactly. The Birth of Athena was a useful metaphor for what it felt like to birth a thirteen-year-old girl into adulthood, but it was an exaggeration, a distillation: like all myths, it was larger than life yet told a truth about it, one that mere autobiography, mere nonfiction, mere real life, could not. You could say the same thing about portraiture, Kate thought. You could never get at the complexity of what it was like to be Kate, Mother of Audrey, or Audrey, Daughter of Kate, but if you captured even a single facet, in an instant in time, you might just capture . . . what? A hint of what it was like to be human, flesh and blood, of what it was like to be alive.

Kate had done many portraits over the years—her mom as the Hopi Spider Woman; Colleen as Circe, Aphrodite, Joan of Arc; herself thinly disguised as any number of benign and malignant beings—and she was not ashamed when she thought of most of them. Among the members of her family, only her brother had managed to escape the wrath of her dowel. Or rather, her attempts at rendering Luke had always landed in her garbage can of recycled clay. He had virtually been her only sibling these past ten years, something of a father figure to Audrey, especially when Sam had first left, and the one person in whom she'd confided, occasionally, when she'd needed a sympathetic, nonjudgmental ear. And yet whenever she'd tried to sculpt him, she'd failed. Something had always been missing in her portraits of him, some secret, key ingredient of his self. Instead of Luke, she'd simply sculpted a man with an angular, Don Quixote jaw. A man with a tuberous nose, pointed chin, cloudy eyes. A tall, thin man with wire-rimmed glasses and a stooped back.

She thought of him now as she deepened the lines of her eyelids with a pin tool, because while Luke's eyes were a different color from hers, and myopic, they had the same long, narrow shape and heavy lids. She took in her progress: something was wrong with the outer corner of the right eye. It was pointed too far up just a fraction of an inch, but enough to skew everything, to make the face unbalanced. A hum of frustration formed in her mind. She leaned back and stared through the bubbled windows at the sky: a wash of blue interrupted by fluffy cumulus clouds, the kind she and Luke and Colleen used to try to identify lying on the beach when they were kids. That one's a unicorn. That one's a train. That one's a mermaid sunning herself on a rock. They were so fluffy, so thick, those clouds, they seemed to have a texture to them; if she stepped outside, she imagined, she could grab a handful of one and hold it to her chest like a cuddly kitten.

She turned to the face in front of her, and spritzed the

corner of the eye with water, smoothed it with her forefinger, then picked up her dowel. She formed a curved line, carefully, ending at a point parallel to the inner corner this time, and did the same with the bottom lid. She was working effortlessly, her fingers motile appendages, her mind a blank page, the cloudless sky of her morning's dream. All she had to do was trust her hands. All she had to do was get the lines and curves right, and things like fear and pain and love would take care of themselves.

To *create real art, one must fall into a trance.* This was what Kate's painting teacher used to say, and at the time, like the other jaded nineteen-year-olds in the class, Kate had thought he was full of it. He probably had been full of it, but as the years had passed, she'd come to understand what he'd meant. She did fall into a kind of trance when she was working, albeit without the lit candles and prayers to the Muse her teacher had recommended, but an absorbed thoughtlessness, a detachment from her surroundings, nonetheless. When the phone rang, she was so intent on pricking a tear duct that she nicked a jagged line instead. "Damn," she muttered. It was going to be her mother, telling her to pick up beer or Coke or Ben & Jerry's on her way over. As long as she'd been interrupted, she took in the face: tear ducts (she would have to smooth out that line), a few final touches here and there, and then (how had this happened?) her own face would be complete.

She might even be able to finish the figure of Audrey by the end of the day, she was thinking, as she wiped her hands on a damp rag and picked up the receiver. "Yeah."

"May I please speak to Kate?" a man with a raspy smoker's voice asked.

"Yes, this is she."

"Kate. I tried calling your mother, but she wasn't home. José Hernandez here. I own the Ocean View Apartments. Your brother's landlord?"

Kate struggled to picture the man with whom she'd talked only a few times in the fourteen years Luke had lived in his building: short, stocky, a cigarette dangling from his mouth as he trimmed a California palm. "Oh, yes. Mr. Hernandez. Hello."

He cleared his throat. "There's no easy way to say this. I'm sorry. Your brother . . . he committed suicide. I . . . I'm so sorry."

Kate had to repeat his words to herself to make sure she understood what he had said. Her first thought—which seemed incontrovertible—was that there must have been some mistake, and she told this to Mr. Hernandez. There's been a mistake, she said. You must have called the wrong number, someone else named Kate. My brother is Luke. Luke Flannigan.

"I know," he answered softly. "Luke Flannigan, number nine. I found the body myself. There was a will on the dining table, in his handwriting, same as on his checks. The police are still in the apartment. They want to talk to you later, but I said to them, 'It's better if I tell the family. They know me.' Listen, I'm sorry, very sorry."

As the man spoke, and Kate found herself less and less able to believe that he wasn't talking about Luke, she felt a slowing down, a numbness throughout her body. He was saying something about moving Luke's things, he was hoping to rent the apartment by the first? and something about the cat. Yes, she heard herself saying, we'll come get the cat sometime today.

"I'm sorry," he repeated. "Your brother was a good tenant. An excellent tenant. I'm sorry."

An excellent tenant, Kate thought, an excellent tenant.

She turned off the phone.

Shadow

The projector starts rolling, the film begins: A summer day at the beach. Mary Flannigan is wearing an unbuttoned cardigan over her white Esther Williams one-piece, as she sits in a lawn chair reading *The Wall Street Journal*. She looks up, gives a quick sailor's salute, two fingers triggering off her temple, and returns to the paper. To her left, in front of the ocean—deep marine blue, with white-foam caps, children up to their knees, a few body-surfers, waves crashing on the shore—Luke and his sisters are building a sand castle. Luke, who is seven, could be on the cover of a tourist brochure for southern California, with his sun-bleached blond hair and tan skin streaked a dusty white with salt and sand. He is digging the moat, letting three-year-old Colleen help him, though sometimes she just shoves the sand back where Luke has dug it out, while Katie, already a budding artist at four, carves a lattice design into the roof. The three of them look at the camera and wave. Then they turn to one another and, after a wink from Luke and a nudge from Katie, zealously kick the castle with their legs and swipe it away with their hands, laughing, as though the only reason they built the thing in the first place was to have this gleeful moment of destruction. Their mother comes up behind them, shaking her head, bemoaning the fate of the beautiful castle, or perhaps she's simply disgusted by how dirty they are. She says something to her husband, something that looks sharp and stern, a command, and briskly walks to the camera. After a brief visual jumble—sand, sea, sky, their mother's sunburned feet—Grady Flannigan appears, ambling toward the ocean. He is a big, lumbering bear who has somehow wandered onto the beach wearing Hawaiian-print swim trunks. The children run after him like eager puppies. When they reach the shore, they pounce on their dad, who falls to his knees, and then, cautiously so as not to squash anyone, rolls onto his back. Katie and Colleen each straddle a thick thigh, while Luke sits atop his father's broad chest. He raises his fists into the air, victorious, and tosses his head back and laughs.

It's a winding road, full of twists and turns and hills, the one Luke's father takes from La Ventura, the next town up the coast, one month later, to their house on Avenida del Sol. Luke can almost see him skirting the freeway entrance to drive down this road, the way he always does, because it's right above the ocean, and his father loves the fresh, breezy air and expansive view, the endless stretch of blue water and pink sky in front of him, after a youth spent among rolling hills, narrow rivers, and dense pines.

The woman in the Cadillac has been drinking. According to the article in *The San Pablo Press,* she's been drinking for two days straight when she drives head-on into his father's Ford, and she is so limber from inebriety that she will survive the crash to walk right out of her car and light a cigarette. Luke's father slams on his brakes and is hit from behind by a moving van filled with heavy antiques, English bone china, and Persian rugs. The speeding Cadillac and the weighed-down truck together squeeze the Ford into an accordion. His father isn't wearing a seat belt—he never does; he's a big man, and claims they're uncomfortable—but that doesn't make much of a difference, since he isn't thrown from his car but crushed between the steering wheel and the seat. The wake and funeral are closed-casket. His father's face, apparently, isn't fit for display.

Everything Luke knows about the ceremony he's gleaned from overheard conversations. He himself doesn't attend the wake or the funeral or the reception afterward: he's too sick to get out of bed. It begins with only a mild nausea and a slight headache, but by the night of the funeral he's sleeping on a comforter in the bathroom, weak from dehydration, his head pounding, his bowels empty and sore; he is unable to distinguish between the events going on around him and his sometimes vivid, sometimes shadowy dreams. He has a vague memory of going to the hospital (but no, his mother later tells him, Dr. Freeman came to the house); of his sisters bringing him a handful of little dead bunnies and a cup filled with heavenly chips of ice; of his mother, in a long white dress, telling him that it was all a mistake, that Daddy's downstairs, and wants to see him. And then he's in the living room (he has no memory of how he's gotten there), where he sees a bunch of strangers (his father's brother and sister and their spouses, who have flown in from Wisconsin), and he's saying, "Where's Daddy? Where's Daddy? Where is he?" and one of the women looks at him and begins to cry, and then his mother ushers him back upstairs and into bed. Later that night, or maybe it's the following night, she sits beside his knees and puts her head in her hands and just sobs, asking Luke what they're going to do without his father and why didn't God take her instead, and then telling him that he mustn't worry, that Daddy is with Jesus in heaven and they should be happy for him, which she is, she is, she's just feeling sorry for herself, that's all.

A week after his father's death, Luke awakens in the middle of the night and knows he's no longer sick. The normalcy that is the absence of nausea and pain feels almost blissful, and it occurs to him that perhaps his father's death was merely some terrible, feverish dream.

It's dark outside—almost black—but inside, some lights are on, and Luke follows them down the stairs and into the kitchen. His mother is sitting at the pine table, a Snoopy mug in one hand, the local paper in the other. Her copper-red hair, which is usually pulled neatly into a bun, falls below her shoulders; her eyes are determined, hard, and unforgiving, the way she looked when Katie and Colleen broke her antique crystal vase. Luke steps closer, and sees that she's reading the classified ads. Something brittle and rocklike forms in the center of his chest, and it's difficult for him to breathe.

"Luke. What are you doing out of bed?" his mother asks,

coming over and pressing the back of her warm hand to his forehead. "You're cool. How are you feeling?"

"Okay, I think."

"You must be starving. How about something to eat?"

Luke sits down in one of the wood-and-straw kitchen chairs. His stomach is hollow, but it's not an emptiness that can be filled with mere food.

He points to the newspaper, to the black circles his mother has drawn around various descriptions under the heading "Accountant," and says, "Are you going to get a job?"

She looks surprised, and then she nods. "I was always planning on going back to work, you know, after all you kids were in school. I'm just going to have to do it earlier than I expected."

She sounds a little angry, and that makes Luke think of the drunk driver. It's too painful; he pushes the thought away.

"Mom? Do you think Dad's . . . you know. Happy?"

"Of course he's happy," his mother snaps. "What's he got to not be happy about? Don't you worry about your father. Your father's just fine. It's me and you, we're the ones who're left to suffer." Her mouth wrinkles at the word "suffer," a bitter lemon, and she shakes her head. "But your father's looking down on us, watching over us, and so is God, and we'll be fine too."

Later that night, after Luke has gone to the bathroom and brushed his teeth, and washed his face for the first time in a week, and basically put this moment off for as long as possible, he's lying in bed in the dark when he can't avoid it any longer. The dreaded words come into his mind: *My father is dead.* The sadness that follows this admission is so absolute he feels dizzy, as though the earth has been knocked off its axis (which it has) and he is flying in black, gravityless space (which he is), and he thinks he's going to cry—his throat aches and his eyes sting. But he can't. He won't.

He stares at the fluorescent galaxy he and his dad cut out of plastic and glued to the ceiling last summer, and imagines his father looking down on him, watching over him, as his mother said. "Dad?" Luke whispers, gazing heavenward, at the lime-green stars. "Which one's Orion again?" He waits for his father to answer. He waits for what seems a long time. The house is quiet and still. The bedroom window is open, and he can hear sparrows rustling in the oleander bush below. "Dad?" Luke repeats. He's tired, but patient; he has all the time in the world to hear his father's good-natured reply.

But his father never answers him, not even in Luke's sleep, when he dreams that he's caught in an ocean undertow, trying with all his might to swim against the tide back to shore.

Sharp stomach pains; a cough he can't quite shake; a pounding behind the eyes: in the months and years after his father's death, Luke experiences strange symptom after strange symptom. At first, his mother, accustomed to catastrophe, imagines the worst—a ruptured appendix, leukemia, a brain tumor—but Luke has been to the family doctor, an internist, a neurologist; he's had blood tests, urine tests, a nausea-inducing CAT scan, and no one has ever found anything wrong. So now, when he wakes his mother one morning to tell her there's a lump in his throat, she places the back of her hand on his forehead and sighs.

"Go back to sleep," she says.

"I can't. My throat," he barely squeaks out. It isn't a pain that you get with a cold, or even strep—it's a lump, a lump he can feel on the inside, as though a Super Ball had somehow lodged there, making it ache every time he has to swallow, every time he has to breathe, and on the outside as well, a swelling the size of a peach pit. He takes his mother's warm fingers and puts them against his neck. Her eyes become wide, afraid.

"Jesus," she says. It isn't a swear word but a prayer. She gets out of bed, hurriedly puts on her robe. "Jesus, Jesus, Jesus. I've got to call— No, he won't— Luke, honey, get back to bed, I'll come get you when we're ready."

Two and a half hours later, after they've dropped Katie and Colleen off at school and gone to Dr. Freeman's office, they're in the car, driving down Pacific Boulevard, toward the ocean, a cool, salty breeze floating through the open windows, to the office of a throat specialist who can see them right away. Cancer of the esophagus, he heard his mother say in the hall outside Dr. Freeman's office. Was she asking a question, or repeating, with disbelief, a reply? Luke doesn't know. He thinks "esophagus" is a fancy name for throat. He wonders if this is what he has; he would like to have something with a name, finally. He imagines a white room: kindly nurses bringing him milk shakes, his mother and sisters worrying beside his electric bed.

"Want a Life Saver?" his mother asks now, at a stoplight.

Luke nods. He's nine years old, the good patient, the patient son. He lifts a cherry one from the top of the roll. He sets it on his tongue, tastes the tart sweetness, and waits. The juices fill the back of his mouth, and then he can't take it any longer—he has to swallow. He steadies himself, and does. The sweet juices are soothing, like a cool hand on a hot forehead. He touches his neck: still there.

"A little better?" his mother asks. Luke nods. "I had an aunt, Aunt Tilly, who used to get terrible headaches," his mother says, her voice laced with the bitter, far-off tone that always creeps in when she speaks about her family or her hometown, which she refers to as Nowhere, Illinois. "She swore the only thing that helped was inhaling lemons. She'd cut one open—or no, she'd make my mother cut it open for her—place it under her nose, and breathe in."

"Other symptoms?" Luke asks, though it's difficult for him to speak.

"No, she just had the headaches. All her life. They got so bad she took to bed one day and didn't get up again for a year."

"Then she was better?"

"No." His mother frowns. "Then she died."

Most of his mother's stories about her family are like this: depressing, pointless, ending in death.

Inside the Pacific Medical Complex, Dr. Jones touches his neck, looks down his throat, takes an X ray, finds nothing, does a biopsy, which hurts, and says she'll call when she has the results. At home, Luke's sisters admire his bandage and bring him hot tea with too much honey, the way they like it themselves. His mother does her accounting in her study and spends a lot of time briskly saying everything will be fine. Luke thinks that just the fact she says this so often is proof it won't be, but he isn't complaining—his throat stops hurting after three days, and still he gets to miss another two days of school. That's his limit, because then the results from the biopsy come in: benign. Two weeks later, the lump is gone, vanished overnight, just as it came.

His mother goes to church that evening to thank the Lord. Luke isn't especially relieved. He knows there will be other mysterious symptoms, other aches or lumps that have no name.

One day—it's summer, a Saturday, Luke is ten—his mother has taken them to the beach. Katie and Colleen have grown bored with splashing in the water, and so Katie, the mastermind, says, "Let's bury Luke," to which Colleen, the loyal strongman whose only rebellion is to one-up her big sister, replies, "Yeah, let's bury him alive."

The sand is cool beneath his back. His sisters have dug out a clearing near the shore and are now piling sand on top of his legs, his torso, his arms, while he lies there motionless, a faithful dog allowing himself to be tortured. It's a warm day, almost hot. Seagulls glide overhead. There are no clouds in the sky, only a pale overcast—no color at all—and a hazy, smog-covered sun that makes him feel leaden. He closes his eyes. He hears his sisters' voices. "No, Colleen, not his face." "Why not?" "Because he won't be able to breathe." "We'll give him a straw." "No, you're gonna get us in trouble." They're right next to him, but they sound far away, as if he were hearing them from deep below the sand.

Once he's buried (except for his face: Katie has won that argument, and Luke is relieved), he feels a heaviness that begins inside his chest and stretches to his limbs—and something else. A dark force of some kind, lurking beside him, eyeing him carefully, ready to strike. Luke is afraid—very afraid—he's hot, his forehead is dripping with sweat, it's hard for him to breathe, he cannot open his eyes, the roar of the ocean is loud, ferocious, menacing.

"I told you not to . . ."

". . . your fault he . . ."

". . . answer us?"

"We have to . . ."

"Mom?"

". . . here."

"Luke? Luke, honey? Can you hear me?"

His mother's voice. He feels lighter now, cooler. A hundred spiders are running up and down his skin. He opens his eyes. Everything is blurry at first, and then he sees: a beautiful day at the beach, his mother and sisters wiping off the last bits of sand from his body.

Luke sits up. Two teenage girls walk by carrying surfboards, staring at him over their shoulders, whispering into each other's long hair. Katie looks worried, and more than that, downright scared; Colleen seems merely curious, the way she was earlier in the day when she poked a stingray washed onshore to see if it was still alive.

"Luke, angel," his mother says, her face anxious, her voice shallow and cracked, "are you okay?"

He'd like to tell his mother what's happened, but he doesn't have the words, and even if he did, he knows they'd sound silly, like a nightmare about vampires relayed in the safe light of day.

"I'm fine," is all he can say. He wants to assure her, protect her, and more than that, protect himself. "Really, Mom. I'm fine."

And he is. He tries to be, anyway. His mysterious symptoms don't vanish completely, but he no longer reveals them to anyone. He tries to be normal. He observes other boys to see how this is done: he imitates their jaunty walk, their raucous laughter, the style of their jeans. He studies hard, does well in school, reads for fun—Bradbury, Greene, Hemingway, Simenon—and in his junior year of high school, falls in with a coed group of like-minded nerds. They go out for pizza together on weekends, watch reruns of *Star Trek* in Trina's family room, swim in Joe's pool, even get stoned together once, as an experiment, though Luke's lungs burn so badly he's relieved when no one wants to do it again. He even goes to the senior prom. Anthony is the only one in their group who has a girlfriend—a junior at another school—which leaves the rest of them (three girls and three guys), and since they're all too chicken to ask anyone out, after a general discussion they draw names from a popcorn bowl to see who goes with whom. Luke draws Cathy, a girl with a wry sense of humor who's planning to study music at some liberal-arts college in Ohio. He smiles. She smiles. They're just friends.

Prom night. The night you're supposed to lose your virginity (if you haven't already), and some people, including Anthony and his date, have taken a hotel room expressly for this businesslike purpose. Luke isn't hoping for anything, but he isn't not hoping either, and once, during a slow dance, he slides his hand down Cathy's spine and lets his fingers wander over a soft round cheek of her taffeta-covered butt, until she stiffens and firmly pushes his hand up to her waist. Luke is gentleman enough to understand that a firm push of the hand means "No chance, buddy," and so after they all go to Denny's, and Luke drives Cathy home, he walks her to the door, gives her a chivalrous peck on the cheek, says, "Thank you for a most enjoyable evening. Good night," and gets into his car and drives home.

It's three a.m. He heads straight for the kitchen and opens the fridge out of habit, stares at the leftover lasagne for a second but then remembers he has two eggs, some hash browns, and about a half-dozen sausage links sitting in the pit of his stomach, and closes the refrigerator. He goes into the downstairs bathroom—"his" bathroom, since the medicine cabinet in the one off the upstairs hallway is filled with his sisters' ponytail holders and headbands, Kate's paintbrushes, and Colleen's bottles of suntan lotion and he couldn't fit in his toothbrush and shaver if he tried. Usually he just peeks into the mirror long enough to see if there's food between his teeth or blood all over his chin, but now—perhaps because the sight of him in a tuxedo is so rare, and he has to return it tomorrow—he sets down his toothbrush and studies his reflection.

"Don't you look handsome," his mother told him earlier that night, beaming proudly, adjusting his bow tie, while Kate snapped pictures and Colleen whined, "I wanna go too." And from his quick glance in the mirror, he thought she was right: He did look pretty handsome, didn't he? But now he sees that he and his mother had only been fooling themselves. His hair is the color of water after a stack of dirty plates and greasy pots have been washed in it. His nose is large, shaped like a yam; his skin ruddy, dotted with a few stray pimples. Why are his sisters so beautiful, and he so . . . so ugly? So hideous? A monster. He splashes his face with cold water, wipes it on a towel, and looks into the mirror again. *This is me*, he says to himself, resigned. *This is my face.* There's nothing much he can do about it.

In college, girls don't seem to mind. In fact, his awkward sincerity, his obvious inexperience in matters of love, actually attract certain women to him, and he finds himself using his reputation as Sensitive Virginal Solitary Man to his advantage, subtly implying through glances, half-smiles, and carefully chosen words that if any girl were to take pity on him, he would treat the act as gratefully as if he'd been saved from drowning, and she would forever glow in the knowledge of having released eighteen years of pent-up lust and Catholic guilt, and of having done him the ultimate favor of becoming priestess to his acolyte, and initiating him into the mysterious world of sex.

It happens sophomore year. One evening, as he's walking to his study carrel in the library, the door to an office opens, and Luke sees the graduate student who was the TA for his class on Shakespearean romance the semester before.

"Good evening, Bernadina," he says, giving her a lustful smile, and then looking down.

"Luke," she answers flatly. "I want you to see something."

Luke is surprised, because even though he often passes her here, between his carrel and her office, at this time of day, they haven't really conversed since last semester.

He steps inside. "What is it?"

Bernadina locks the door, closes the blinds, and begins to unbutton her blouse. It's dark inside the book-filled room, but Luke can see her breasts swelling over her red satin bra, and he instinctively covers his crotch with his books to hide his growing erection. She unzips her jeans, revealing a soft, fleshy belly and wide hips, and steps out of them, kicking some books away with her feet. Then she unhooks her bra, pulls down her underwear, and says, "Come here."

Whether it's shock or desire or some combination of the two that paralyzes him, Luke doesn't know, but it takes all of his energy to let his books fall from his hands and move toward her. Bernadina unceremoniously takes off his clothes, unrolls a sticky rubber onto his penis, pulls him to the carpeted floor, and straddles him with her thick, voluptuous thighs, relieving him of the burden of his virginity before he has time to touch her breasts. It isn't until afterward, when they're lying side by side, their sweaty bodies an inch or so apart, that Luke thinks to kiss her on the mouth.

"Let's not get sentimental," Bernadina says. "This was nothing more than a final exam."

Luke isn't sentimental: he's grateful, from the center of his chest, which jumps for days afterward every time he thinks of her, to his skinny calves, on to which Bernadina held so tightly at the moment of climax that her jagged nails drew tiny points of blood from his neophytic skin. He's grateful not only because Bernadina realized for him an adolescent fantasy he never imagined would occur in real life, but also because the experience—brief and nerve-racking as it was—has inspired in him a feeling of supreme accomplishment. *I am a man,* he says to himself as he shaves, as he lies in bed at night, as he buys a cup of coffee from the snack bar girl with the beautiful burgundy hair.

Two weeks later, when a scrawny, myopic woman—who turns out to be a transfer physics major named Lucy Green—meanders into the first-floor lounge to borrow coffee, instead of simply handing her his can of Folger's, Luke smiles and asks if she'd like him to make her a cup. They sit side by side, sipping coffee, chatting about relativity and *Siddhartha* and what they're doing for spring break, and something unusual creeps into the warm, still air between them: an electricity that could have been formed only by lust. With her boyish figure, baggy clothes, and oversized tortoiseshell glasses, Lucy has the mien of a mousy intellectual fourteen-year-old, a Girl Scout and perhaps future troop leader, asexual as a dictionary. But as they talk, Luke notices her jutting clavicle, an artwork of almond-colored skin and protruding bone, her wide, moist lips, and her endearing manner of hugging her legs between her arms and occasionally kissing her bare knee, a gesture of self-loving that makes Luke warm with desire, and furious at the ungrateful joint.

When two guys from down the hall come into the room to play chess, Lucy scurries away. The following evening, Luke calls to ask if she'd like to join him for dinner. She tells him she's busy, and Luke assumes that they'll become little more than acquaintances, that whatever charge he felt between them was entirely of his own making, or imagining. Then two nights later, he hears a determined knock on his door. He sets down his French book and opens the door to find Lucy, a good foot and a half shorter than he, standing in the hallway. From her hungry eyes and twitching fingers, Luke knows immediately why she's there. "Lucy," he says. "Won't you come in."

The months that follow will forever be engraved in Luke's memory as the semester of his debauchery. He maintains his grades, remains sober and industrious, continues to go home twice a month or so to mow the lawn and do laundry; but nearly every day, he or Lucy knocks on the other's door—in the morning before classes, in the afternoon just before dinner, in the middle of the night—to engage in a bacchanal of earthly pleasures. Lucy may have the demeanor of a Girl Scout too shy to sell her troop's dreaded cookies, yet there are times when Luke suspects she only plays this role so that the shock of her pantherlike passions will be all the more arousing. They're college students who attend classes and write papers and are respected by their professors, but together, they are The Insatiable Lovers, leading secret lives of new positions, pleasure condoms, and four-letter words neither of them uses in everyday life, even when they stub their toes or discover they owe twenty dollars in overdue library fines. They don't discuss their childhoods or their unhappy high school years or what they want out of life; they are a man and a woman without a future or a past, who say, *There, Harder, Faster, Slower, Giveittomebaby, Not yet.*

Their liaison ends as quickly and unexpectedly as it began. Two weeks before the end of the semester, Luke starts devoting himself to studying for finals and writing papers, immerses himself in scholarly pursuits. He supposes that Lucy must be doing the same, because one afternoon he realizes they haven't seen each other in eight days—which would have seemed an impossible eternity just the week or so before—and he can't remember who knocked on the other person's door last. The next morning he sees her eating by herself in the cafeteria, her head buried in a thick science textbook while she gnaws on a chocolate-covered doughnut. He carries his tray to her table and sits down across from her. When she looks up at him—there's a smudge of chocolate on her cheek—she smiles. It's the smile of an eighty-year-old seeing a man who was once her lover, a long time ago, and who still thinks of him now and again, with fondness. Their relationship has simply died of its own accord, like a poinsettia after the holidays.

There are other women after Lucy, a dozen, fourteen, sixteen, maybe more, a frantic quest for more women, more, more, more, women whose lips he will never forget but whose names he will never recall, women who comfort him, excite him, use him, and one—a Canadian with badly bitten nails and talented pink feet—who falls in love with him. Luke isn't interested in love. Or rather, love isn't interested in him. For as much as he'd like to fall in love, get married, unite himself body and soul with another human being, he doesn't believe such a thing is possible. Not for him. Not yet. Perhaps not ever.

Which is too bad, because all this soulless sex, this making love without feeling any, with women about whom he will never, ever dream, is wearing him down. He's always tired, yet he can never sleep. Or else he falls asleep at one and wakes up three hours later, bleary-eyed but wide awake. Sometimes he finds himself perusing a row of books in the cavernous library, studying the call numbers, searching for something, only he can't remember what. He forgets about women for a while and throws himself into his work. Then one day the shadow appears.

It's morning, and he awakens filled with dread. Light is streaming through the yellow curtains his mother bought for his dormitory single; birds are chirping wildly in the cypress tree outside; music floats in from down the hall: the B-52's singing, "Twistin' 'round the fire, havin' fun . . ." He's a senior; it's April; everything is happy, chirping, and light. But he feels something lurking beside him, watching him, something dark and menacing, a force, like eyes, boring into his head. He's too frightened to move. He tells himself not to be ridiculous, and goes to take a shower. The warm water rushing over his body soothes him. He thinks, I really need to cut down on the caffeine.

Yet as he walks home from the library one night a week later, there it is: a sensation of dread throughout his being, the certainty that something is following him. He turns around. No one is there. Or in his Hardy seminar: a tingling in his limbs, followed by numbness, a sinking in the pit of his gut. He keeps looking over his shoulder, but of course there's only the white, undecorated wall. Is he going crazy? Becoming paranoid? Surely part of insanity is not knowing that you're insane, so as long as he suspects he's going loco, he tells himself, he should be all right.

Luke has been trying to sleep since one. It's close to four and he's simply lying there, exhausted but wide awake, no longer even trying, studying in his head for an upcoming philosophy exam, when, suddenly, he knows he isn't alone. He sits up in bed and looks around. The room is dark, illuminated only by a distant streetlamp. The window's open; his curtains are billowing. The air was hot and still all day, the sky a yellowish hue, and now a Santa Ana is blowing in, a hot, easterly wind that's whipping a branch on the cypress back and forth against the dormitory wall. In the distance, a dog howls. Luke hears footsteps, then a voice: "Should we order a pizza?" It induces in him a shudder; the guy might as well have said, *The world is ending right now.* He closes his eyes. Breathes in, breathes out. When he opens his eyes he sees a shadow on the wall beside his desk. It's the rough shape of a human, standing, and Luke stares at it, terrified, transfixed, until it moves: something like an arm makes a slow arc, waving good-bye, or perhaps hello. Luke glances behind himself, but no one is there. When he looks again at the wall, the shadow is gone.

One day not long before graduation, his mother calls and says, "Luke, I want you to come home. Your sister has eloped."

Naturally, Luke thinks she means Colleen, because Kate is in art school, and even though she did bring home a charming mechanic for Easter dinner, Luke believes that this Sam fellow is nothing more than a mild rebellion against artsy bohemian oppression, and that one day, when she's thirty or so, Kate will marry a fellow sculptor, or a curator, or an editor for *ARTnews* who falls in love with her during an interview. Colleen, on the other hand, could drop acid, fly to Vegas, and come home married to a waiter or Barron Hilton at any time.

"With whom?" Luke asks.

"Sam Monroe, who else?" his mother says. "A few weeks ago I had the audacity to ask her if she didn't think she was getting too serious, and didn't she want to date someone at school, and well, you know Kate. This is her way of telling me to mind my own business, because there's not a thing in the world I can do now—except have a little dinner reception for them at the house tonight. Can you be home by five?"

"Well . . ."

"Ooops, I have another call. See you tonight, honey. Drive carefully." And with that, she hangs up.

The atmosphere at his mother's is hushed and disappointed, as though someone nobody was all that fond of suddenly died, ruining everyone's plans for the weekend. Colleen mopes around the house in a black halter dress, a sexy young widow in mourning, obviously furious at Kate for abandoning her by marrying Sam Monroe. Their mother keeps shaking her head, stumped by some persistent internal question, presumably: Why did her nineteen-year-old level-headed daughter go off and marry a mechanic she's known for only eight months? Kate appears pale and dazed, as if she went to sleep drunk and woke up with a thin gold band on her finger, unaware of how it got there or why this man who fixed her Honda Civic last October is referring to her as his wife. Sam Monroe is the only one who appears to be in his element. He glows with contentment as he narrates to Luke (having apparently already told it to Colleen and their mother) the story of the elopement, how a few days before, he asked Kate to marry him right then, and how they hopped on the back of his motorcycle and drove to the court-house, because if you know something is right, why wait?

He gives Luke a boyish grin, a turning up of the mouth that then spreads until even his cheekbones and nose seem amused, a smile that takes delight in the world, and includes you—the person at whom he is smiling—in this Gatsby-like delight.

"I need a cigarette," Colleen says. "Anyone care to join me?"

There's a short silence—Luke can hear someone grinding coffee beans in the kitchen—and then Sam says, "I'm too comfortable to move," and the funny thing is, even though they're in the living room, where they never go unless it's a holiday or they have company, Sam is sitting in such a way that he makes the stiff formal couch appear comfortable.

Kate nestles her head into the crook of his neck. Colleen glares at Luke.

"Oh," he says. "Yeah, I could use some fresh air. Excuse us."

Outside, Luke sits in one of the cushioned patio chairs while Colleen leans against the wooden rail across from him, stretching her tan legs in front of her, holding a glass of champagne in one hand, an unlit cigarette in the other. Her hair—long, wavy, honey-blond—is down, and looks unruly, as though she hasn't brushed it all day, which she probably hasn't. While her peers are constantly washing their faces, bodies, and hair, and spending hours in the bathroom applying makeup and using curling irons, Colleen has never given up setting her alarm clock for twenty minutes before school begins, and she's forever leaving the house tying her hair in a knot, slipping sandals on her feet, trying to get the dirt out from under her nails with a toothpick or a book of matches.

"Don't you just hate Sam Monroe?"

Luke is taken aback by the extremity of the verb, because only this past Easter, Colleen joked with Sam over dinner, flirted with him mildly, casually, the way she might with her married phys. ed. teacher, seeming to enjoy his company just fine.

"No," Luke says. "Of course I don't—"

"You know what really gets me?" She gazes into his eyes, as if she's speaking to him, and not—as he often feels—to herself.

"What?"

"Not only didn't she call me beforehand, to tell me she was getting married, to maybe even ask me to be a witness, because, you know, you'd think she might want her sister to share in her wedding? She didn't even tell me afterward. Mom did. I mean, Kate called here at the house, and told Mom, and never even asked to speak to me."

Luke doesn't know what to say. He respects Kate's desire for privacy and wouldn't have expected her to call him at school on her wedding night to tell him the news herself, but it is odd that she didn't confide in Colleen. Then again, his sisters' relationship has always been inscrutable to Luke.

"It doesn't matter, though." Colleen nods instead of shaking her head. "She'll see. I'll get married myself one day, and I won't say a word about it to her until I'm back from my honeymoon, and then she'll know how it feels."

The back door opens; their mother steps outside. "Come on, kids," she says glumly. "They're going to cut the cake."

As Kate and Sam dig a knife into a white cake decorated with chocolate roses, they gaze at each other with what looks unmistakably like love. Kate seems to have come out of her stupor and remembered exactly why she agreed to ride on the back of this man's Kawasaki and vow to love and cherish him until death does them part; Sam looks at her with wonder and amazement, as though she's the first woman he's ever seen. When they tenderly stuff cake into each other's mouths, Luke feels that he is watching an unfamiliar tribal custom. How can they know, at nineteen and twenty-one, with whom they want to spend the rest of their lives? Grow old? Raise children? Love through sickness and health, in poverty and in wealth? How do they know that what they're feeling is indeed love? But they do know, it's obvious to Luke that they do, and he's awed by their certainty and courage.

Later that night, after Sam and Kate have left for a long weekend in San Diego because they can't afford a honeymoon in Hawaii or Cozumel, and Colleen has gone out, and their mother is upstairs in bed, Luke goes into the backyard. He walks over the longish grass (he'll have to mow it tomorrow) and sits under the avocado tree, whose glossy leaves shade the deck. It's a warm night, and the trill of crickets and the scent of jacaranda blossoms fill the air. Luke leans his head against the trunk, surveys the tangle of pale branches, and knows, before he looks down again, that the shadow is there, on the grass. He isn't surprised. He's been waiting for it to reappear since that night in his dorm room, and now he feels frightened, yes, but inside this fear is something like its opposite, its upside-down twin: relief. There's a sense of *At last.*

He lowers his neck so that he's looking straight ahead, and blinks. He realizes now that he was expecting something else— his father, come back to haunt him after all these years—but what he sees is not his big bear of a dad. It's a boy. A boy with black hair, pale, pale skin, and dark rings around huge, intense eyes. His hands are in his pockets, his back is hunched, but he doesn't look sullen, exactly, more like dead, and somehow resurrected—unwillingly, Luke thinks. He stares at this apparition, and it stares back, unblinking, and walks toward him, slowly. If Luke were able to move he would run and never stop, but he can't move, he can't even breathe, all he can do is sit and wait to see what happens next. The boy is crouched in front of him. His eyes are sad, but also accusing, as though this were all Luke's fault. Luke feels like apologizing, but knows this is unnecessary, because he knows—he's known since he first saw this boy— that they are the same, the ends of a single piece of rope tied in a knot. He reaches out his trembling fingers, but they merely glide through the air.

"This," he whispers softly, "is who I am."

Lost in Flight

Audrey woke up to Courtney Love longingly droning "I want to be the girl with the most cake"—the clock-radio alarm was set on KROQ. She felt kind of nervous and excited, as though it were Christmas, or her birthday, and remembered she had a cross-country meet that day, an away meet at Sepulveda. She pulled down the covers, twisted open her wooden blinds and looked out the window that faced the street—Mrs. Grant was watering her lawn; the Epsteins' cat was sauntering along the sidewalk, like a teenage boy with his hands in his jeans pockets, hopefully looking for trouble—and decided that it was perfect running weather: a little cool, a little misty, but not chilly, not downright wet. She went to her bookshelf, turned her Magic 8 Ball upside down, then right side up, asked, "Will today be a good day?" and read: "Signs point to yes."

Today will be a good day, she told herself. She would ace her Spanish quiz, look in the bathroom mirror to find that no pimples had erupted during the night. Blaine Durbin wouldn't just smile at her or say "Hey" when they passed in the halls between third and fourth period; he would stop and talk to her, maybe even ask what she was doing that night, did she want to come and hear his band, and she would be very James Bond, as Sandira would say, and tell him maybe. Mr. Monotone would be sick and they'd have a sub in geometry, somebody cool enough to make the theorems sound as interesting as they really were, when you weren't in that stuffy classroom but at home, using a protractor and a compass. And most important—even though the same inky phrase had surfaced on the Magic 8 Ball last Thursday, when she'd raced against La Ventura and come in third—she would win her cross-country meet.

Audrey had always loved to run. Her mother joked that she had learned to run before she'd learned to walk—that she'd needed to swing her arms back and forth, gaining momentum, before she could move—but her mom kind of liked to idealize her childhood, so Audrey wasn't sure whether this was true. But she did remember that she'd preferred running in and out of the ocean when she was little to swimming in it, and she'd always been—if she did say so herself—fast. She liked to sprint, to create that rush of wind and pump her legs as fast as she could, but what she really loved, and what she was best at, was distance. That peak feeling that would come over her a couple of miles into her run kept her doing it, day after day.

She'd tried to explain the sensation to her uncle Luke one time, after he'd asked her what she liked so much about running, but it wasn't the sort of thing you could easily articulate. The pain crept out of your legs and chest so that you weren't even aware it was happening, and then you felt like you had no legs, like you were gliding, bodiless, weightless, euphoric. The euphoria was hard to talk about without sounding really sappy, even though you didn't need to worry about sounding sappy with Uncle Luke. It was like all the stress of school and home and friends and boys and what you were going to do with your life floated away, and you were left with this sensation where every little thing—a yellow daisy, a certain slope to the hill, the smell of the ocean, a cloud, a memory you had of when you were sick and your mom brought you OJ and smoothed back your hair—made you happy to be alive. Some days it didn't happen at all—she just felt slow and sluggish, her legs could have weighed a hundred ten pounds each—but three times (she could remember each one clearly), she'd experienced it in the extreme. Those three times made up for every shin splint, sore muscle, wobbly knee, and minute of nausea she'd felt: those times, she'd felt like she was flying.

She put on a pair of running shorts and a tank top, then went into her mother's room. It was empty, which was weird, because her mother never got up before she did. For a second she felt almost panicky, but when she went into the kitchen and saw the coffeemaker on, she knew her mom was around somewhere. She made herself a blueberry smoothie, then opened the door between the kitchen and the studio. Her mom was sitting in front of this big clay head balanced on a neck, looking kind of dazed.

Her mom was just not a morning person. She didn't eat

breakfast until lunchtime, or shower and change into real clothes until everyone else was coming home from work or school. And her idea of exercise was to go for a nature walk where you stopped every two feet to look at some bug or a plant. She'd probably seen Audrey leave the house a thousand times wearing shorts and running shoes, but she always looked at her like she didn't understand why anyone would run unless she was being chased, especially before noon. In fact, no one in their family—at least no one she had ever met—was very athletic, which had made Audrey wonder if she'd gotten her running abilities, like her light brown eyes, from her dad.

"Mom?"

Her mother looked up, and said good morning, and then followed Audrey into the kitchen and started to tell her about some stupid dream she'd had, but Audrey really didn't want to hear it. "Mom, quit dreaming about me," she said, because this was maybe the millionth time her mom had dreamed about her in the past month, and Audrey was getting sick of it. It was like, all day long her mother talked to her and asked her questions and grilled her about her classes and friends and what books she was reading and her views on everything from *Seinfeld* to the death penalty, and knowing she was in her mom's unconscious as well as her conscious mind all the time made her feel like she was being stalked.

When her mom poured herself a cup of coffee, Audrey sat down at the table and opened her Spanish book, because Friday was the day of their weekly quiz, and even though they were being tested on regular -*er* verbs—easy as Eskimo Pie—Señor Ramirez always threw in a few totally obscure vocabulary words, like *ingeniero* or *cuadrada,* just to be sadistic or something, and Audrey wanted to be prepared.

"Remember, it's Friday," her mom said.

Audrey rolled her eyes, because she knew it was her mother who had just remembered it was Friday—her mom always forgot what day it was, not because she was scatterbrained, she wasn't, but because she lived in her own ceramics world and mostly had no reason to keep track of things like days and dates and sometimes even months—and said, "News flash, Mom, I know." Then they talked about whether Audrey would go with her mom and Uncle Luke to her grandma's for dinner the way they always did on Fridays, or whether she'd go out for pizza with her team, and Audrey could tell her mom wanted her to eat with them by the way she said, "Okay, just let me know," in this forced, easy-sounding tone, and just for that reason—because her mom tried to sound like she didn't care, not because her mom wanted her to come—Audrey thought that maybe she'd go out with her team. But thinking that made her feel a little sorry for her mom, and she decided that maybe she'd call her for a ride after all. The thing was, as much as her mother sometimes drove her crazy, Audrey felt kind of good when she was around.

Audrey heard the beep-beep of Missy Springer's Subaru, gathered her stuff together, and ran outside before her mom could corner her for some big, corny good-bye, like she was going off to fight for oil or democracy or something, instead of just leaving for school.

Missy Springer was a pothead. Every morning, as soon as they turned the corner out of the condominium complex, she lit a joint and smoked it, with all the windows down, until they got to the student parking lot at school. While they were driving the mile and a half there, Audrey sometimes wondered what would happen if a cop pulled them over, but Missy always seemed about as worried as a professional cat burglar or something. She was a junior who lived on La Paloma, the street by the swimming pool, and ever since Audrey had made the cross-country team, Missy had taken her under her wing, telling her what to do if she got a cramp and yelling, "Go, go, go!" at her during practice. Which had turned out to be kind of an honor, because the amazing thing was, even though Missy always ran stoned, she was easily the fastest girl in their school, maybe in the whole conference.

About a month before, after they'd been riding together for a week, Missy had handed Audrey the joint. It smelled sickly-sweet, and felt funny between her fingers—thinner than she'd expected, and a little wet—and for some reason Audrey became really scared. Her fear embarrassed her, and she tried to bring the joint to her lips and inhale, at least once, just to see what it was like, but her hand just wouldn't move to her mouth, and she gave it back to Missy, feeling like a total geek.

The next day, Missy hadn't even bothered to pass her the joint. And since then, Audrey had sensed that Missy was disappointed in her, like she'd given Audrey this gift that Audrey didn't appreciate or something. Their car rides had become quiet, but not tense; it was more like they'd reached some limit to their relationship, some freshman–junior, passenger–driver, running protégé–running goddess limit, which in fact suited Audrey all right. She had enough problems without worrying about what Missy Springer thought of her.

Not that she lived in Sarajevo and had to dodge snipers all day, or that she was a black guy in some urban ghetto whose primary goal was to see twenty-five. But still, San Pablo High School was its own little world, with its own little pressures and mores, and if you didn't fit in, or didn't get it, you would be marked forever.

Every person you talked to, every outfit you wore, every smart or not-so-smart answer you gave in class was another drop in cementing who you were. Everyone used to think of her best friend Sandira as a real schoolgirl, but then she'd dyed her hair a rusty red, pierced her nose, and started hanging out with Mark Ruiz, and now people didn't know what to think. When Sandira ate lunch with Mark for the first time, Audrey stood on the steps overlooking the outdoor area of the cafeteria and felt completely lost. Should she go over to Lisa Walker, who was half white and half black and who she used to be really good friends with, but who wanted to hang out only with a certain African-American crowd now that they were in high school? Or this girl Megan in her physical science class who seemed really nice, but who she didn't know all that well, and who was eating with a bunch of her own friends? Audrey had felt so exposed standing there, like she didn't have a friend in the world, and then this cool artsy girl Trisha walked by and told her she liked her pants, and Audrey asked her how she'd done on their English quiz, and pretty soon they were taking out their sandwiches and eating together, right there on the steps.

That had been a small victory. But for every one of those it seemed there were a million failures. Like the time she'd been faced by this jock because she'd given a long-winded answer in English and afterward Brad Spiner had said, right in front of everyone, "Damn, who's the teacher here?" and Audrey had wanted to melt into her seat and just vanish. Or the time she'd talked to Blaine Durbin for about ten minutes after lunch one day, and she'd felt pretty hip in her smiley-face T-shirt and flared jeans, but then this guy Warner came up and asked Audrey if she could help him install more memory in his laptop, and she could just see Blaine's eyes glaze over like, Oh, a computer geek. It didn't help that she was thirteen—she'd skipped third grade and was a year younger than most other freshmen—and everyone probably knew it, because how could they not, when all the other girls had breasts and hips and she was lanky as a boy. And it also wasn't exactly a point in her favor that she was a runner. Especially one of the best. It was one thing to be a cheerleader, or to play basketball, or even to be on the volleyball team, which was still considered cool—but it was another thing to run cross-country with skinny dweebs like Bruce Paisley and Shannon Brown, and be good at it. Sometimes she felt she was teetering on the verge of becoming categorized as some baby-brain cross-country freak. And the worst part of it was, she was afraid that Sandira was bailing out on her.

It wasn't just Mark Ruiz and the fact that Sandira had a sort-of boyfriend and she didn't, or that Sandira and Mark seemed to have all of these secrets and private jokes that made Audrey feel like a little kid peering down the stairs at a cocktail party or something whenever she was with them. It was also the way Sandira had changed her image overnight, getting her nose pierced and dyeing her hair and spending her back-to-school clothes money on baggy pants and fitted tees and this black leather jacket she'd found at the Goodwill, instead of going to the Gap or even Urban Outfitters the way they usually did. And she'd done this all by herself, without even telling Audrey, so that on the first day of school, Audrey had been as shocked as the lowest stranger to see Sandira's nose-stud and rusty-red hair and little yellow T-shirt that said "Porn Star." Ever since then, Audrey had been able to tell that it bothered Sandira that she had this witness, this person who had been best friends with her since fourth grade and knew that she'd once had a crush on goofy Tom Lyle, and that after she got off the phone with her dad, who lived in Iran, she always, always cried, and that ever since she was in the womb or something she'd wanted to be a civil rights attorney, someone who knew that this nose-ring, Porn Star, dye-job business was just some pretentious affectation and who wasn't about to drool all over her like some of the other kids, who were like, "Sandira Hafiz is so cool."

They were still friends. They still got their periods on the same day and ate each other's food without asking. They still talked on the phone nearly every night and saw each other most weekends. But until last summer, they'd used to tell each other everything, without even thinking about it, and now it was like, they always thought first. It was a subtle shift, not the kind of thing anyone else would easily notice. Grandma, Alek, even her mom, still thought they were the best of friends, as close as they'd ever been, and they all tried to make Sandira feel comfortable about her transformation—her mom had gone so far as to say she liked her "new maroon hair." But Audrey would never forget the day her uncle Luke had seen The New Sandira for the first time.

Audrey had been waiting with Sandira in her grandma's driveway for Mrs. Hafiz to come pick her up, when Luke had come over carrying a bag of grass to set by the curb.

"Hey, Uncle Luke," Sandira said.

Luke stared at Sandira and pushed his wire-rimmed glasses up his nose. "Excuse me," he asked, "but who are you?"

"That's Sandira!" Audrey said, laughing. Her uncle must have seen Sandira a million times, and had even taken them both to the father-daughter breakfast in eighth grade, since neither of them really had a father.

Anyone else would have said, "Oh, Sandira, sorry, I didn't recognize you," but that was the thing about Uncle Luke. Even though he lied sometimes, it wasn't the way everybody else did. Other adults were always lying to you in this way that was supposed to protect you or something, but Uncle Luke was the most honest person she'd ever known, even as he was lying. So when he set down the bag, cocked his head to the side, and finally said, "You're not Sandira," it was like he was telling the truth while pretending not to recognize her.

Sandira looked kind of embarrassed. She smoothed back her hair with her hands like she could turn it black again, but all she did was call attention to the silver rings on her fingers and thumbs. "Yeah. It's me. Sandira."

"You're sure about that now, are you?" he asked, and Audrey laughed—because he sounded so earnest, and because he was like the kid who said the emperor wasn't wearing any clothes, and Sandira was like the emperor, ashamed and pissed off to be walking around naked and have some little kid point it out to her, after everyone else had been fawning all over her invisible new duds, and because it was just funny to think of spending two hours in her grandmother's house with this girl who may or may not have been her best friend of five years. And even back then she'd known it was kind of sad, but no matter how hard she'd tried, she hadn't been able to stop laughing.

Audrey gathered her books and stepped out of the classroom into the noisy hall. Her legs were tight from her run a few hours before, and she was hungry—it was nearly lunchtime—or maybe the hollow sensation in her stomach was just nerves. Because it was here, after third period, in front of the water fountain, where she usually saw Blaine Durbin. Sometimes he stopped and talked to her, and sometimes he didn't, and she never had any idea or any control over which it was going to be.

She caught a glimpse of black curly hair, pale skin, and then the girl in front of her stopped at a locker, and there he was, coming toward her, his gray eyes looking beyond her at someone or something else. She was staring at him, smiling at him, she had worn her navy miniskirt and black tights and brown plaid shirt just for him, just for this moment—"Hey, Blaine," she said—but he didn't hear, he was passing her, he had passed her, he was gone.

"Well?" Sandira said, when Audrey got to the locker they shared.

"He didn't even notice me. He walked right by. Or maybe he did notice, and pretended not to."

"Let's not be paranoid," Sandira said, gazing into a pocket mirror, applying powder-blue lipstick. She was wearing a Mr. Bubbles T-shirt that read "Makes Getting Clean Almost as Much Fun as Getting Dirty" and a bunch of plastic baby barrettes in her hair. Sandira had dark, dark eyes, perfect olive skin, and full lips, and once, when they were about ten and eleven, a talent scout had handed her his card at the mall and asked if she wanted to be on TV, but Sandira had told him, "Sorry, mister, this kid's not for sale."

Now she smacked her frosted lips together and inspected her teeth. "Why are you always waiting for him to talk to you? Why didn't you go up to him?"

"I said hi. What am I supposed to do, tackle him in the hallway?"

"If you want a guy, you have to go after him. You can't just wait around like some passive groupie. I mean, he's a junior in a band, not Leonardo DiCaprio. You should just, I don't know, give him a call."

"Give him a call," Audrey repeated. "And do what? Hang up the phone when he answers, the way you used to with Matt Bukovich?"

Sandira stuck out her jaw and rummaged for something in the locker. "That was a long time ago," she said.

"Oh yeah, ages. Let's see, the prom was in May, that's . . . what? Five months?"

"God, Audrey, get a life. A lot can happen in five months. A lot can happen in a week."

This was Sandira's way of reminding Audrey of something she alluded to so often that Audrey couldn't have forgotten it if she'd been given electroshock treatments like a million times. Back in July, Sandira had gone to Catalina for a week and slept with a college guy from Colorado. She may not have changed her look until September, but it was back then, in the middle of summer, that she'd begun to act different, practically grown-up, possessing some secret knowledge now that she'd entered the world of beer commercials and music videos and every song on every radio station and the way older guys looked at you at the beach. And maybe because Audrey was already grumpy because of what had happened with Blaine, and because sometimes Sandira and her naughty little T-shirts just bugged her, Audrey said, "A week? It didn't take you that long to become a *woman,* did it?"

Sandira gave her this smile of total disdain, as if Audrey had just tried to wound her by throwing a marshmallow at her. "At least I'm not a virgin," she said.

Sandira had already walked away before Audrey had the wits to mutter, "I'd rather be a virgin than a slut," and the guy whose locker was next to theirs—this total dork who had this old Madonna picture taped to the inside of the door and who was always checking to see if they were looking at him, which they weren't—was like, "Right on!" And Audrey just wanted to bang her head against the metal locker.

She put away her *Four Shakespearean Classics,* grabbed her African-American history textbook, and walked up the stairs to her fourth-period class, where she saw Alek standing in front of the door. "Audrey," he said, "can I speak to you for a moment?" and these girls Mercedes and Amber were all, "Ooooh, Audrey, Mr. Perez! Go for it, girl!" because Alek was, like, the faculty heartthrob.

"What's wrong?" she asked. His face looked troubled, and besides, they had this unspoken agreement not to bug each other at school. Usually when they saw each other in the halls or the lunch area they said hello, but they never really talked, they never let on that they knew each other—that they used to have foot fights or that he had taught her how to downhill ski or that once he'd told her if he ever had a daughter he would want her to be just like her—because it was bad enough just having him around, invading her privacy, knowing who the cool people were and who were the dweebs and probably having a pretty good idea that Sandira wasn't the sweet, innocent girl her mom still thought her to be.

"I'm just here to give you a message from your mom. She asked me to tell you that she's going to pick you up at Sepulveda High after your meet today, okay?"

"But Coach Bryant's taking us out for pizza."

"I know—that's why your mom's picking you up. She wants you home early tonight."

"But why?"

The bell rang, and Alek said, "I've got to go. I'll see you at the house, okay? Oh, and good luck with your race." He squeezed her shoulder and hurried down the hall. Audrey knew that she should walk into the classroom and sit down before Ms. Shepherd gave her a tardy, but it was nice to stand in the quiet, empty hall, and she was transfixed by Alek's back. She felt a little annoyed at her mom—not because she wouldn't be able to go out with everyone for pizza, since she didn't mind being quiet and alone for a while after she ran, and because it was Friday and Uncle Luke would be coming over for dinner anyway, but because her mom hadn't given her a choice in the matter. It was like she had just decided that Audrey should come home early and had made Alek tell her and that was the end of that. Not that she blamed Alek, though—he was just the messenger. He was just this double agent, working for both sides, who tried to respect Audrey's privacy and not get in her face too much but who probably got grilled by her mom and could easily tell on her if she ever ditched school or held hands with a boy, neither of which seemed very likely at this point. Audrey felt kind of sorry for him. He was always holding back, trying not to intrude, trying to be her friend, because he couldn't be what he really wanted to be—her father.

Audrey watched him disappear at the end of the hallway and then sneaked in the back door of the classroom.

Audrey already had a father. Samuel Jacob Monroe. She'd learned his middle name in seventh grade, when they'd done a social studies project on family trees, and she'd taken her sheet of paper with all the blank boxes to Uncle Luke, who hadn't needed to ask her why she hadn't taken it to her mother or grandmother instead. The next day, he'd given her the answers over the phone. Or most of them, anyway. Her father, it turned out, didn't know when his father was born, or what his middle name was, or whether he was dead or alive, because he'd left before Sam had been born. (Maybe, she'd often thought, leaving your wife and kids was a trait that ran in the family, like light brown eyes, athleticism, and a mechanical ability.) But she'd learned that her father was born in Olympia, Washington, that his mother, Frances née Olsen b. 1931, still lived there, and that he had an older sister named Helen, who had a husband and two boys. She had written in all of the spaces on either side of the tree—she'd had to monkey with it a little, because Aunt Colleen was on both sides, and so was Sam Monroe, which was kind of embarrassing, like they were incestuous hillbillies or something, though Mr. Yamamoto hadn't said anything about it— colored the branches and leaves, earned an A, and then hid it in the shoe box filled with a bunch of old letters under her bed so that her mom wouldn't find it, like it was a dirty magazine.

When Sandira's father had up and gone back to Iran, Sandira began to ask her mother a million questions about their breakup, like why he'd gone back to Iran and how come they'd separated and whether they were ever going to get back together, because even now they weren't officially divorced, and her mom was like, "You ask too many questions!" but she always answered her. Whereas Audrey had always gone along with her mom and pretended that she'd sprouted from her rib, or that she'd been a test-tube baby from some anonymous donor. Between her and her mother, it was as though Sam Monroe had never existed. There were no pictures of him, none of his belongings, not even a stuffed animal that had been given to her by her "Daddy," and Audrey might have believed she'd never had a father if she didn't remember this feeling that came over her when she used to ask, "Where's Daddy? When are we going home?" and something inside her mom would vanish and not return for a long time. She'd hated that feeling, as if she were all alone in the world when her mother was only a few inches away, and so at some point she'd stopped asking.

Besides, what was there to ask? Audrey knew—she'd probably known even when she was three—that her father had simply left. There were times when she'd been sure that he'd come walking through their door, smelling like a gas station, smiling and lifting her into his arms, and there were other times when she'd convinced herself that he couldn't find their new apartment, that he was lost, that he kept returning to their old home at night wondering where they had gone. But deep down, she must have suspected something like the truth, because when she was about to enter kindergarten, and her mom had told her that he was gone for good, she hadn't been too surprised. That was the evening her mother had explained—in this totally forced calmness that had let Audrey know she was not at all calm, that her father and her aunt had gotten married and moved to Phoenix right after the divorce, and that if any of the kids at school asked, she should just say that her parents were divorced and her daddy lived far away. And she still remembered thinking, What aunt? because she had no memory of Aunt Colleen and hadn't known that her mom even had a sister, that her grandmother had another daughter, because no one had ever talked about her or even mentioned her name. And at the time, this knowledge—that there was some female equivalent of her uncle Luke in the world, someone she hadn't known existed just a few seconds before—had seemed weirder to her than the fact that this person, this *aunt,* was married to her father. Which definitely did seem weird to her, once she got a little older.

Her uncle went to visit her father and aunt every once in a while, and it was after one of these trips—the last her uncle had taken—that he'd handed her a silver bracelet and said, "This is from your dad."

Audrey didn't know when it had begun, or how—had her uncle just one day volunteered the information that she in fact had a real live dad? Or had Audrey asked him about her father the way she used to ask him about everything else, from how do airplanes fly to why do boys try to scare you with bugs when bugs aren't even scary to how come some people are evil, because he was the one person who took even the dumbest questions seriously. But for as long as she could remember, they had talked about Sam Monroe easily, or as close as you could get to easily when talking about someone who'd helped create you and then never bothered to send you a card on your birthday. Her mom was, well, *her mom,* and her grandma was the closest thing she had to a second parent, and Alek was like some perfect would-be substitute dad who made sure you knew what had happened at the Battle of the Little Bighorn and how to patch a tire on a bike, but Uncle Luke was the person she could talk to about anything. It was like he saw everything more clearly than other people did, more deeply. He reminded her of one of the angels in *Wings of Desire,* always kind of lonely and sad, which made sense, because if you were more perceptive than other people, if you walked around like one of those brooding angels who hung out in libraries and saw into the nature of reality or something, why would you be all sociable and happy?

Audrey took the bracelet—a solid silver band with two cats' heads coming together at the opening—and slipped it onto her wrist. Then she met her uncle's eyes. "I don't get it."

They were sitting on her grandmother's deck. Her uncle leaned back in the patio chair. "We were shopping, and your father pointed to the bracelet and said, 'I bet Audrey would like this,' and I said, 'Yes, she is rather fond of cats,' and then today, just before we were about to leave for the airport, he handed it to me and told me to give it to you."

Audrey thought for a moment. "Can I tell Mom it's from you?"

"I am the one who actually put it in your hands."

"Uncle Luke?"

"Yes?"

"Why this? Why now? I mean, he never gave me anything before."

"I suppose it reminded him of you."

"But he doesn't know me. How could anything remind him of me?"

"Because he's your father."

Luke looked away, as if he knew this was a lame reply, and they didn't say anything else. Audrey stroked the silver ears of the cats until her grandma called them in for dinner.

When she and her mom went back to the condo that night, Audrey wrote her father a letter. She'd been writing to him since fourth grade, letters on stationery printed with dinosaurs or seashells or kittens playing with string, which she addressed, stamped, and vowed to mail, but which she always ended up putting in the shoe box under her bed. They were a record of her life: She began by introducing herself, telling him that she liked horses and watermelon and the smell of anise on the hills by the ocean where they sometimes went for walks. In her next letter, she mentioned her new friend Sandira, who could beat everyone in their class at jacks. At ten, she told him that her mom had a new boyfriend, a really nice guy named Alek Perez who seemed to know everyone in San Pablo and who had taken them to Disneyland and had bought her a really cool cap. After the Christmas when Uncle Luke had given her a pair of Sauconys and she'd begun to run, she wrote about her favorite trail, above the cliffs overlooking the ocean, where she could try to go as fast as the seagulls in the sky, which everyone else said were just beach pigeons but which she kind of loved. In seventh grade, she'd told him that her mom had come down with pneumonia, and Alek was staying with them for a while, making soup, and taking her to and from school, and she confessed that she wasn't afraid of spiders or heights or even rats but that the idea that her mom would someday die made her feel like a little kid lost at the fairgrounds or something, and asked him what he was afraid of.

The letter she wrote the night Uncle Luke gave her the bracelet she'd even gone so far as to carry all the way to the mailbox the following morning. She'd stood on the corner, holding open the blue swinging door, and she'd almost dropped the letter in, but at the last minute, she'd turned around and walked home with it, and then stored it on top of all the others. It was still there, ready to be mailed, in case she ever got up the nerve.

Dear Dad,

I was wondering if maybe you wanted to come out here so we could talk to each other in person. No one would need to know. We could meet in the lobby of the San Pablo Hotel. You'll know me because I have your eyes, and my mother's mouth and pale skin, and freckles on my cheeks and the bridge of my nose, that I think are just my own. And then we could go into the lounge and have piña coladas or something. I mean, mine would be virgin, of course. I'm almost twelve now, so you don't need to worry about me causing a scene. I've never been much of a crier.

Because I was just wondering, if maybe after we sat

down and ordered our drinks or whatever, you could tell me why. That's all I want from you. I just want you to look me in the eye and explain to me why you never sent me a Christmas present or called me on my birthday or came here and took me out to breakfast. You wouldn't have needed to take me anywhere fancy, just a diner, or the beach, just someplace where we could have talked. But now, all I really want to know is, Why? Like, what was it? Did I cry too much? Did I have a bad temper? Was I sick all the time, or were you disappointed because I wasn't a boy? Did you come home from work and want to relax and I was always bugging you to play with me, or maybe it was the opposite, maybe you'd try to hold me and I'd run away? Or maybe I watched cartoons really loud or screamed my lungs out when you were trying to sleep? Wasn't I nice enough? Smart enough? Pretty enough? The thing is, whatever it was, I wish you'd just tell me. Because then it would be like, Okay. Now I know.

Audrey

I can, I can, I can was the chant of her feet—the right was *I*, the left *can*—now that she'd passed the four-K marker and had only a kilometer left. Her legs were still tight, even though she'd jogged a lap before the race and had stretched, and the tightness kept her tied to her body, to its pain. She shook out her arms, wiped the sweat from her forehead, and concentrated on the red jersey in front of her, willing herself to move closer to it. There were three Sepulveda girls between her and Missy Springer, and all she had to do was kick into high gear and pass all three of them, one by one. She ran harder, faster, but the girls ahead of her were running faster too, and when it was time to sprint up the last hill and then coast down, the tightness in her right calf became thicker, knotted into a cramp—Shit—and she could feel someone coming up behind her, now at her side, Sharissa Johnson, a teammate. They were running side by side, they were at the top of the hill, Audrey could see the finish line—I can, I can—and then Sharissa pulled ahead of her, and Audrey came in sixth.

She bent down to massage her leg, and felt a hand on her back. Coach Bryant was looking at her with a mixture of sympathy, curiosity, and disappointment. "I'm sorry," Audrey said. "I don't know what happened. I tried."

Coach Bryant nodded. "I know you did." That was one of the things Audrey liked about her coach. She didn't tell you "Nice race" when she knew you could have done better.

Audrey was stretching her calves when she spotted her mom off to the side of the small crowd. She walked over to the finish line, where she congratulated Missy and stood around with everyone else to see the end of the race. She knew her mom was waiting for her, but she thought, Let her wait, and watched Becky Whately-Smith run against a girl from Sepulveda to see who would come in last. Everyone from San Pablo was chanting, "Beck-y! Beck-y!" and everyone from Sepulveda was yelling, "Cin-da! Cin-da!" and it was silly, because what difference did it make who came in last, but it did. Nobody cared who came in seventeenth or third-to-last, but nobody wanted to be dead last. "You can do it, Becky!" Audrey yelled. She liked Becky Whately-

Smith and felt sorry for her because she was pretty slow and a little overweight but she tried so hard. Her pink cheeks were going up and down as she ran, and at the last minute, she pulled in front, and beat the Sepulveda girl by about an inch. Everyone went over and hugged Becky so hard you'd have thought she'd come in first, and then the judges finished averaging the times, and the San Pablo girls had beaten Sepulveda by sixteen seconds. Audrey told Coach Bryant she was leaving, grabbed her bag, and walked toward her mom.

Her mother was wearing corduroy pants and a gray cardigan and her brown boots—Sandira always said she looked like someone in a J. Crew catalogue who was staring out to sea with a dog at her feet, and it was true that she had this kind of classic eastern look to her that made Audrey proud whenever she had to introduce her to someone.

As Audrey got closer, she noticed that her mother's eyes were puffy and red, and her skin, which was usually smooth and pale, was blotchy, like it was when she had a bad cold. "Mom?"

Her mother put her arm around her. "Hey, you did pretty good, huh? Sixth?"

"Sixth isn't that good."

"There must have been about thirty girls running. I'd say that's pretty good."

They walked into the parking lot, and Audrey asked, "Have you been crying?"

Her mom kind of smiled. "I told myself I had to stop before I came to get you, and I did, but then I cried again in the car on the way over. I didn't want to worry you."

"What's wrong?"

"Let's get into the car and I'll tell you, okay?"

When they were sitting inside the car, the unspoken thing was just hanging there, and it made Audrey nervous. She tried to think of what could be wrong, what could have happened— she had never seen her mother cry before in her life—but she couldn't think of anything, and the not knowing was awful, it was like this terrible weight that she just wanted to go away, even if the knowing would be worse. "What is it?"

Her mother looked into her eyes and held her hand. "Your uncle Luke is dead, Audrey," she said quietly. "He killed himself."

Audrey's hand felt trapped. She didn't want it there, under her mother's, but she couldn't take it away, and even though she was staring straight ahead, she could feel her mother's eyes on her, which made her feel like a bug under glass, or like an actress in a play. Her mom moved her hand to rub her eyes, and Audrey crossed her arms over her chest and looked out the half-open window. Shouts came from the course, and she knew that the boys were finishing their race. They were trying to come in first or second or break their times, and their parents and teammates and friends were rooting for them to win, and Uncle Luke was dead, he had killed himself, his body was probably in some morgue. He must have been dead while she had been running too, while she'd been riding over on the bus, sitting in all of her afternoon classes, because he must have been dead when Alek had told her that her mom would be picking her up. They'd kept it from her, postponed telling her until after she'd finished her race, and it made Audrey feel weird and manipulated to know she'd had some false ordinary day, when her uncle had taken his life. She looked over at her mom. She wanted to say something, but her mom looked like she might be on the verge of crying again, and Audrey knew it would be petty to bring it up.

"How did he . . . You know. Do it?"

"He overdosed on sleeping pills."

Her mother said this gently, and Audrey nodded. Knowing that he'd just fallen asleep and not woken up was kind of a relief.

"Do you feel like talking?" her mother asked.

Audrey shook her head. It was like, What was there to say?

When they pulled into the driveway, her mom said, "I guess I should warn you about Grandma."

"What do you mean?"

"Well, she isn't speaking. I don't think she's said two words to me since I told her, and she refused to talk to the police when they came to the house." She turned off the ignition and added, "Maybe you can try talking to her. Maybe she'll open up a little with you."

Audrey didn't really feel like getting out of the car, but her mom had already stepped outside and was looking at her, so Audrey followed her into the house. Usually at this time of day on Friday, things were banging around in the kitchen and the news was blaring, but now everything was quiet and still. Audrey set down her bag and walked with her mother into the living room.

Her grandma was sitting in the armchair by the window that

faced the street. "Can I get you anything, Mom?" her mother asked. "Water? Tea?"

Her grandma didn't say anything, didn't even seem to hear. Her mom squeezed her shoulder and gave Audrey this worried look that was like, See what you can do, and then walked through the dining room and into the kitchen.

Audrey stepped a little closer. Her grandmother's eyes were wide open, tearless. They weren't even red or puffy like her mom's, as if she'd been crying on and off all day. They looked lifeless somehow. Her jaw was hard, set, and her skin was a raw, pasty color. Audrey had heard the expression "aged overnight," and she realized this was what it meant. It was like looking at a different person, someone who had the same features as her grandma, but who was years older. She reached down and touched her hand.

"Grandma?"

Audrey waited for what seemed like a couple of minutes. Her grandmother didn't give any sign either way whether she wanted her there or not, and finally Audrey left.

"Any luck?" her mom asked, when she went into the kitchen.

Audrey shook her head.

"Hey." Alek came over to her and put his arms around her, so that she had no choice but to lay her cheek against his chest, which felt kind of good, actually—she could hear his heart, ba-boom, ba-boom, it was soothing, and his flannel shirt was soft—and then he broke away and said, "You all right?"

"I'm thirsty," she told him.

"Let me get you some water."

"I can get it." She poured herself a glass of water from the Brita pitcher in the fridge, and then stood against the counter, sipping it.

"Are you sure you want to do it tomorrow?" her mother asked, as Alek sat down across from her.

"I'd just as soon go ahead and get it over with."

"Because José said he wanted it done by the first, which gives us plenty of time. Or maybe he said he wanted it rented by the first. I can't remember."

"Look, tomorrow, next week, it doesn't matter to me. I might as well do it tomorrow when I go to pick up the cat."

"The cat," her mom repeated. "We'll have to get food, and litter, and what else do you need for a cat?"

"Kate, don't worry about it. I'm sure Luke left some supplies, and whatever we need, I'll get. You have enough to worry about."

"I have to start making calls. People should be coming home from work by now. Did you phone the bakery?"

"Yeah."

"How many coffee cakes did you order?"

Audrey set down her glass and went upstairs. Maybe it was a delayed reaction from running, or maybe it was from listening to all this talk about cat litter and coffee cakes when it was like, her uncle had just killed himself, who cared whether Alek had ordered three coffee cakes or four, but whatever it was, she was beginning to feel kind of sick. She knew that she should take a shower, but instead she went to lie down on the thick denim comforter in "her" room—the room she slept in whenever she was at her grandma's.

When her uncle was little, he'd had a glow-in-the-dark galaxy of stars stuck up on the ceiling, and she could still see the white shadows they'd left behind. Now each one was the question Why? It wasn't a question filled with outrage or shock. Not like if someone had told her that her mom or Alek or Grandma or Sandira had killed themselves. Then the Why? would be like banging your head against the wall, it would be a murder mystery that had to be solved, because she knew that they would never kill themselves in a million trillion years. But with Uncle Luke, even though she didn't really understand it, even though she'd never suspected he'd been that depressed, in a weird way she could look back on his life, on the way he'd been, and think, Oh. Not quite Oh, I get it. Just Oh.

A couple of years before, two kids from her school had killed themselves in a double-suicide pact. The boy had played on the football team, and the girl had been pretty and smart, and also religious—she was president or something of the youth group at her church—the kind of people you think have everything going for them. And then a month before eighth-grade graduation they'd jumped off the cliffs at Lookout Point.

Audrey had been to those cliffs a thousand times. There was a lighthouse there, and a nature trail, and a really nice picnic area, but mostly, it was the place where everyone went to watch the whales on their migration from Alaska to Mexico each year. There were telescopes and a chalkboard with the number of sightings for each species, and a visitors' map with pins stuck in places as far away as Ecuador and Japan. Audrey and her mom used to go there with binoculars and hot chocolate early in the morning and look for the blows—they had seen blue whales, gray, killer, as well as dolphins and sea lions—and had gotten to know the other regulars pretty well. But after those kids had killed themselves, people started going there just to see where they'd done it, taking pictures and gawking like it was a Hollywood tourist stop. The story had even made it to the tabloids: "Modern California Romeo and Juliet Plunge to Their Deaths for Love!" a headline had read. Once Audrey had seen some middle-aged women carrying that newspaper, pointing to the spot, taking pictures.

Because at first that's what people were saying. That April's parents were against the relationship because they were religious and were afraid it was getting too serious, and that they'd forbidden her to see Lang anymore, so that the two of them must have decided the only way they could be together was if they were dead. Lang's mother and all his friends said that it must have been April's idea, while April's parents and all her friends said that she would never have done such a thing if Lang hadn't talked her into it. And at school they'd had this special half-day of mourning and counseling, where there weren't any classes, just these "rap sessions" where they were supposed to share their feelings, and some people said they thought it was noble of them to die for love, but most people said it was really stupid and cowardly and a total waste, and Sandira was like, "Is it okay if we go to study hall if we don't really have any special feelings to share?" and Mrs. Torres had told her not to be insensitive, and a bunch of April's friends had gotten upset. But it turned out that it wasn't really about love at all.

The day after the funeral, April's little sister found the note. *I don't want to hurt anyone,* it had said, *I just want to spread my wings and fly,* and everyone had been like, "What kind of a reason is that?" but the more Audrey had thought about it, the more it had made sense. Maybe everyone had this yearning to just leave all the pressures of life behind, like who you were and who you wanted to be and what other people wanted you to be, and whether anyone would ever love you as much as your mother did and why certain people who should have loved you didn't, and even stupid pressures like thinking you were too fat or too thin or your breasts were too small or too big, which you knew were stupid but couldn't stop worrying about just the same, and not-so-stupid pressures, like if someone beat you or raped you or hated you for not being the color or religion they thought you should be, and maybe it had just overwhelmed April, this urge to leave the earth behind and fly away from it all.

Audrey rolled onto her side and hugged the pillow to her chest. She felt strange—hollow, empty, and afraid, and sad in this cold, lonely way that felt familiar, though she couldn't remember having felt like this before—and even though she didn't think her uncle had ever held her, she wished that he was there, lying beside her, his arms wrapped tightly around her back.

The pangs in her stomach felt like a betrayal. She shouldn't be hungry, but she was, she couldn't help it, she wanted something to eat. She walked downstairs, and was about to go into the kitchen when she heard her mother (who was around the corner with Alek, probably at the kitchen table—Audrey could hear them but not see them) say the word "Colleen," which made her freeze in her tracks.

". . . then I suppose I should make up a bed, just in case she comes in tomorrow and wants to spend the night."

"Do you think she will?"

"I don't know. She was too upset to think about making plans."

"I wonder if Sam will come with her," Alek said.

"He won't come. No way. He's much too afraid of me to show his face in this house, I don't care what the occasion is."

"Even after all these years?"

"You don't know. You don't know how I was."

"I know."

"No you don't. Sam isn't coming, believe me."

Maybe, Audrey thought, if she stayed right where she was, she'd become invisible, she'd melt right into the wall, her back would flow into the white plaster, until she became a part of it. Then she wouldn't need to think about anything, or feel anything, or taste the metallic bitterness in the back of her throat. But she could feel her shoulder blades rigid against the hard wall, and the empty space behind the arch in her back, and she knew she wasn't melting into anything.

U p

Four days after Luke has graduated from college and moved back into his childhood home, he's awakened in the middle of the night by a tentative knock at the door. He gropes for his glasses, checks his alarm clock—it's five after two—and says, "Mom? What is it? Come in."

It isn't his mother but an angel who opens his door, bathed in pale luminescence, topped by a glowing halo, and Luke realizes that the light from the hallway and his own semiconscious state are playing tricks on him, and the beatific being with the golden corona is only Colleen, her honey-blond hair piled messily on top of her head.

"I'm eighteen," she says, walking toward him and sitting beside his feet, as though it were two in the afternoon and they had been talking since twelve. "This is the oldest I've ever been, and the youngest I'll ever be." She lets out a laugh that sounds like falling coins. "And I'm bored out of my skull! Mind if I smoke?"

Colleen lights a cigarette and puffs out three white rings, watching the airy clouds until they disappear. Luke used to find this kind of thoughtless self-absorption exasperating, but lately—perhaps because he's further from her than ever, and so can see her more clearly—she's only charmed and amused him, and he rather admires the way she treats life as an entertaining play God has staged for her benefit.

"This is my first summer that isn't summer vacation," she says. "It's the beginning of real life. But it doesn't feel like real life, it feels like I'm still waiting. What if waiting for real life is like waiting for the longest day of the year? You wait for it and then you forget about it and then it's September or something."

Her words sound familiar to Luke, but before he can place them, Colleen asks, "Remember how I wanted to be a nun?" and Luke smiles, recalling how she wore a habit five years in a row for Halloween. She looked so pure and serene, rosary beads in one hand, trick-or-treat plastic pumpkin in the other, trying sweetly to finagle all the M&M's and Blow Pops from Luke's and Kate's bags.

"Yeah," Luke says, "I remember."

"I wanted to be just like Saint Thérèse of Lisieux. The Little Flower." She lies back, stretching her arms above her head. Her short knit dress hikes up her tan thigh, and a peek of white cotton underwear edges into his vision. The image, belonging, as it does, to his little sister, who wore the exact same kind of underwear when she was a toddler and ran around the house refusing to put on her shorts, is as unerotic to Luke as a glimpse of his mother's gray underpants; and yet he can't help wondering if Colleen is teasing him, making a game out of trying to arouse her bookish brother with this seemingly innocent gesture.

"I thought you would be shut up in your cloister with God and you'd have it made," Colleen says. "I wanted to have a passion the way you had your reading and Kate had her art. I guess I do, but God knows it isn't a very saintly one. I wonder if that's why she got married."

"What?" Luke says. Colleen has a habit of expecting other people to read her mind, which tends to work like a beautiful, jumbled poem, full of unexpected leaps, without connectors or prepositions.

"Kate. I wonder if that's why she got married. Maybe she thought it would mean that she wouldn't have to decide anything anymore. I mean, her real life has begun." Colleen stands abruptly and paces around his room, smoking. "God. I've got to get the hell out of here. I have to move out. I really do. It's like being stuck in an elevator, and someone's wearing too much perfume." She laughs, says, "Sweet dreams, Brother Luke," and leaves the room as suddenly as she entered.

Three weeks later, it's Luke, not Colleen, who moves out. He does it for the solitude, the quiet, the space that's his and only his, the ability to read in the evenings without having the TV or Henry Mancini's *Breakfast at Tiffany's* (Colleen's favorite album, which she plays at least three times a day) waft into his room. It's what he's supposed to do: twenty-two-year-old college graduates aren't supposed to live at home with their mother and eighteen-year-old sister; they're supposed to pave their own way, support themselves, begin, as Colleen put it, their real lives.

His apartment is white and bare, with books piled on the floor, the home of a minimalist or a secular monk, or of someone not planning to stay. If anyone were to ask him what he plans to do with his life, he would reply that he wants only to ripen like a peach on a tree. He works full-time at Jerry's New and Used Books on Ninth Street, where he's worked the past two summers, and spends his days trying to turn Danielle Steel aficionados into Jane Austen junkies, buyers of sentimental love poetry into readers of Neruda, Dickinson, and Keats; brewing Turkish coffee and raspberry tea and stocking the tape player with Coltrane, Haydn, and the sound of gray whales blowing; and unwrapping, shelving, dusting, and selling his beloved books. He spends his evenings reading, the way he did as a child, whatever interests him, in whatever order, allowing one book to lead to another like clue after clue in a never-ending treasure hunt in which the hunt itself is the gold, the search the only grail, the reading its own reward: *King Lear* leads to Aeschylus, which leads to *The Birth of Tragedy,* which leads to Dostoevsky and Kafka, which lead to the modernists, beginning with Conrad and, after a seafaring pause at *Moby-Dick,* continue with Joyce. Luke's hope, which he barely dares express even to himself, is that someday he too will be able to write something beautiful, something valuable, "a work of art sprung from its own necessity," but his attempts always seem vapid and awkward to him, and after a stanza or a couple of paragraphs he inevitably gives up. His nights he spends alone—with a single exception. One evening an older woman reaches out to him in her loneliness, a thin, hungry loneliness, wobbly and difficult to bear, a woman with hooded eyes and the most beautiful hands he's ever seen, smooth, slender, veinous, and tanned, and they spend a sad night together trying to console each other with their bodies, but it just makes Luke feel he's cheapened both her and him, and when she comes into the store a week later to buy a cookbook, they hardly acknowledge each other as he rings up the forlorn sale.

Several years pass in this way. Luke is twenty-six. His life is normal, really (no nonexistent shadows cross his wall or materialize in front of his eyes), except that he's having a little trouble sleeping. Well, he's always had a little trouble—he's never been like Colleen, who can fall asleep on the beach or in a car or as soon as she crawls between any sheets, foreign or familiar—but now he's going to bed at eleven, falling asleep at twelve, maybe one, and then waking up at five, four-thirty, sometimes four.

The Ocean View apartment complex (a thoroughly misleading moniker, since expensive condominiums block any view of the ocean a half-mile away) is in the shape of a square. Luke walks along the outdoor corridor, down the concrete steps, past the swimming pool, and through the lit hallway to the laundry room. It's four-thirty a.m. The room is empty, of course. (One of the lesser-known advantages of insomnia: You never have to fight over the two washers and one working dryer.) It's a small room with a concrete floor, a window, and a bulletin board advertising psychic readings and a found Siamese cat. Luke has only a small mound of clothes in his hamper (he did his laundry just a few days ago, but why let it pile up?). He throws everything into one washer—khakis, T-shirts, white dress shirts, boxers; his only darks are socks and a pair of navy sweats too old for the colors to run—adds liquid detergent, and sits down in the yellow Plastiform chair.

The water fills the porthole window, then begins to swoosh around his clothes, creating a white sea-foam of soapsuds. His clothes go around and around, coming together (the sleeve of a white dress shirt entwining with an argyle sock), then falling away. The water is turning gray-brown. Usually this cheers Luke—all that sweat and mud and crusted guacamole washing away from his clothes—but now it makes him feel heavy, burdened.

The fluorescent light above his head emits its relentless, industrial hum. Something starts to ache inside his body, only he can't figure out where. His stomach? His heart? His groin? No, more like his lungs. Not exactly in them, but surrounding them, as though something were squeezing on them from the inside, making it hard for him to breathe. He imagines a boa constrictor wrapped around the luminal ventricles in his chest. He imagines a shaded area of an X ray. He almost feels (but this is absurd) that he's being watched from the inside. He imagines a pair of dark, sunken eyes, staring at him, accusing him. *Why have you returned?* he wants to know, though he isn't sure what he means by "you," except for this lurking feeling, this dark presence, making him nervous and afraid. He places his hand on his chest, closes his eyes, and pictures a gray shadow lurking below the skin. The color of dirty laundry water. Spreading out. Swooshing around.

"I need to talk to you," Colleen says.

His sister has come into the bookstore breathless and agitated, running her fingers through her damp hair. There's no one else in the store—it's two-thirty, after lunch and before school lets out—for which Luke is grateful, since Jerry's New and Used Books has the aura of a library or a warm, friendly church, hushed and respectful, not the place to make a dramatic scene.

"Are you all right?"

She doesn't answer him, but silently paces across the hardwood floor in front of the cashier's desk. She's wearing a skirt and T-shirt that she probably wore to work—she's a receptionist at a public relations firm this summer—and she's perspiring so much that he can see her chocolate-brown bra underneath her pale blue tee. Her hands are like wild kittens she doesn't know how to hold: they hug her chest, throw themselves at her sides, push back her hair, and finally clasp together.

"I think I've just done something terrible," she says. "I have. I've done something unbelievably bad."

With her tangled hair, wild eyes, and wringing hands, she reminds him of Lady Macbeth, and if Luke hadn't heard her say something similar a hundred times before, he would be alarmed. "You haven't killed anyone, have you?" he asks.

This is a joke, of course, but Colleen stops in her tracks and says, "I don't know. I've killed something. I don't know what. Maybe. I just don't know."

"You want to tell me about it?"

Colleen doesn't seem to hear. "I felt like I was in this dream, this terrible, wonderful dream that I kept thinking I would awaken from, but I never did. But I will someday. Someday it will be over and—" She shivers, as if she's caught a chill in the air-conditioned room, and then meets Luke's eyes. "Men are so . . . weak," she says. "It's pathetic."

Luke feels that some response from him is necessary, as representative of this weaker sex, and so he nods. "Maybe you want some coffee," he suggests, proud of himself. This is what people do for others in times of duress: they offer refreshment. "Or tea. I have a nice herbal blend that might calm you."

"I am calm. I'm as calm as someone waiting for the gallows. Someone who deserves whatever happens to her. I feel perfectly doomed."

"Whatever you've done . . ." Luke doesn't know how to finish.

"Can't be that bad?" The cowbells on the door ring; an elderly man Luke recognizes shuffles toward them with a walking stick. "That's the beautiful thing," Colleen continues. "It is. It's that bad. It's the worst. I've done the worst thing that I can do, and now that it's over, I feel . . . I feel . . . terrible!" She laughs, but it's a strange laugh, one Luke has never heard: not the sound of someone charmed and delighted by the performance that is her life, but the macabre creak of a woman on her deathbed who has decided, at the last minute, to make a joke that isn't funny. She pats the counter. "I'll let you get back to work," she says, and tells the old man, "I like your cane," as she passes him on her way out.

It's clear to Luke that something more serious than usual has happened, something Colleen needs help with, and watching her leave the store, he feels inadequate and guilty, a failure in his role of Protective Elder Brother, as hopeless a Laertes as Colleen is an unlikely Ophelia. Perhaps he should run after her. But what would he do? What would he say? Besides, she's probably on her way to Sam and Kate's duplex by now, and will tell their sister, her usual confessor, what she's done, and Kate will know exactly how to respond: she'll sigh, shake her head, try to talk sense into her, maybe argue, and then hold her and whisper "Shh" into her hair while Colleen cries into her arms. When Colleen's tears have run dry, she'll drive back home to their mom's—not for a tearful confession, but to be fed bland food and French vanilla ice cream, to take a long bubble bath, to be told she isn't eating enough, that she should see all the interesting courses offered at the community college next semester, and doesn't Colleen want to learn Spanish or computer programming or even how to make beaded jewelry? And after all of this tough sisterly and maternal love, Colleen will undoubtedly awaken the next day—even this time—feeling like a new girl.

And if her latest sin is somehow beyond consolation and atonement? Luke sighs, suddenly weary. The truth is, he doesn't really care.

It's a beautiful summer day, a Thursday, Luke's day off. What do people do on beautiful summer days? They go to the beach, or to the pool. Luke hasn't been to the pool all summer—not since last year, in fact, when Kate was trying to teach her daughter how to dog-paddle—and he feels pleased with himself for coming up with the idea. Maybe that's what he needs: a little sunshine. Some fresh air. Vitamin D.

He puts on his trunks, his thongs, his terry-cloth robe, grabs *To the Lighthouse* and an ancient tube of sunscreen, and steps outside, where the warm air presses against his lungs.

"Going to the pool?"

Luke turns and sees Mrs. Weiss, his eighty-two-year-old next-door neighbor, outside her apartment door, sitting on a lawn chair and smoking a cigarette. Even though Mr. Weiss has been dead for sixteen years and their two children live in Israel and Missoula, Mrs. Weiss continues to cook for a family of four, and since she also thinks Luke's too skinny, and that men can't cook their way out of a can of Campbell's soup, she brings him leftovers: potato pancakes, kugel, pot roast with mashed potatoes and chicken gravy. In return, he feeds her cat when she goes to Tucson to visit her grandson, and changes her light bulbs, and picks up cartons of Virginia Slims for her when she's run out.

"Yes," Luke says. "It's a beautiful day, isn't it?"

"Gorgeous," she agrees. "You enjoy yourself down at the pool."

Luke breathes in, breathes out, pads along the corridor ("Be sure to wear sun repellent!" Mrs. Weiss calls) and down the steps, and then finds an empty chaise longue. The pool area is crowded with people and noise. Three children are playing Marco Polo in the shallow end. A god-awful sound—arrhythmic heavy metal—comes from a boom box and then stops. The woman beside Luke rubs coconut oil over her tan legs and tells her friend, "No, you don't understand. Tiffany is a magnet for the paranormal." The sunlight burns Luke's eyes.

He thinks about reading, but who could possibly concentrate in this heat ("Marco!"), with all this noise ("Polo!")? He stares at the bright blue water (or rather, the clear water above the brightly painted concrete of the pool) and decides to go for a dip. He removes his glasses, sets them on his rubber thongs, walks to the edge of the kidney-shaped pool, and kneels down.

He trails his fingers in the water, which is always a mild seventy-two degrees but which feels cold against the heat of his hands. The three children are moving through the shallow end slowly, careful not to give away their positions, and as the water becomes still, Luke sees his reflection and is startled. He isn't wearing his glasses, but despite this, or perhaps because of it, he can see his pale face wiggling in wavy stripes. He presses his wet hand to his cheek and feels the arched bone below. That lurking presence hasn't really left him since he first felt it inside him in the laundry room. (Or did he feel it even before then, even when he was a child? Has there ever been a time when it wasn't with him?) *Something is wrong with me,* he thinks, and immediately feels the way he imagines alcoholics must feel when they first stand up at an AA meeting and say, "Hi, I'm Luke, and I'm an alcoholic," and everyone shouts, "Hi, Luke": shocked, ashamed, sad, and relieved.

Something is wrong. Very wrong. Other people don't feel

some phantasmic shadow spreading inside their chests, squeezing more and more tightly against their lungs. Other twenty-six-year-olds don't have jobs that any bright seventeen-year-old could do; they have careers, girlfriends, buddies, the energy to take a shower without needing to gear themselves up. Maybe he's sick. That would explain it: the lack of energy, the sunken cheeks. Anemia, perhaps, or asthma. Maybe AIDS.

He goes back to his chair, puts on his glasses, glances around at the healthy, suntanned people by the pool, and decides that when he goes back to his apartment, he'll make an appointment at the clinic to have some tests. He looks down at his chest (scrawny, pale, with a few black hairs around his sternum, nipples, and belly button; otherwise, he's as hairless as a dolphin or a boy), feels the aching burn below, and imagines his white blood cells trying to fight off the red, the white cells disappearing, one by one, until they're gone.

Ten days later, the test results come in: Negative. He doesn't have AIDS, or anemia, or even asthma. According to the doctor at the clinic, he's fine.

"I'm a failure," his mother says matter-of-factly. "An utter and complete failure as a parent."

A week ago, it all came out: How Colleen began to visit Sam on her lunch break and after work ever since she got the job as a receptionist at the public relations firm a block from Sam's garage; how one day (the day three months ago—Luke understands—when she came into the bookstore, frantic and distraught) one thing led to another, and then another, until Kate walked into the garage just as Colleen was walking out. And now? "We're in love, we're going to live together, we're going to be married. I guess we are, anyway, once the divorce is final. And I feel absolutely terrible about the whole thing."

According to his mother, this is what Colleen said over the phone last week, before Kate even entered their mother's house with her suitcase and a bag of Audrey's toys. "At first," his mother told Luke, a couple of hours after she got off the phone with Colleen, "I thought it was a practical joke. Remember those practical jokes Kate and Colleen used to play on me every April Fool's?" No, Luke said, he didn't remember. "One year they called from a pay phone to tell me I'd won the Publishers Clearing House Sweepstakes, and did I want my ten million paid by the month or the year? Another time Colleen ran into the house shouting that Katie had been abducted by a man wearing a black ski mask, wielding a knife. Don't you remember? I grounded both of them for a week. So all I could think of was that this was just the latest of their sick jokes on me, and I was about to say, 'Aren't you girls getting a little old for this?' But then I remembered. It was September. Not April. Five months too late to be a joke."

It's Luke his mother has been depending upon all week, calling to let him know she disowned Colleen, then calling him again to tell him she wasn't disowning her, but only not allowing her to set foot inside the house; making him come along when she took Audrey on a shopping spree at Toys "Я" Us (apparently hoping that a barrage of talking dolls, neighing horses, and pop-up books would distract her from the absence of

Daddy Sam); and now, before he has a chance to mow the lawn, sitting him down at the kitchen table to tell him that she's a failure.

"In a way, I'm not surprised. My mother died when I was so young, I didn't have much of an example. Not that that's an excuse. I've just been trying to see where I went wrong, and for all I know, it began back then, when I was fourteen and my dad was in a drunken stupor and I had to raise myself. Or when you were babies, still in the crib. See, whenever you'd cry, first thing I'd do was check your forehead to make sure you didn't have a fever. Then I'd check your diapers, then I'd give you the bottle. And if nothing worked, I'd just let you cry. Maybe I should have held you more, I don't know. Or maybe I shouldn't have worked so hard when you were young. Oh, I'm not saying I shouldn't have worked at all, I'd have been a monster if I'd stayed home all day, but maybe I should have made sure I was there when school got out. You, I never had to worry about, and Katie neither, she was always into her drawing. But God only knows what Colleen managed to do every day from three o'clock to five."

Her hands—large, red, farmer's daughter's hands—grip her coffee mug tightly. "I told Colleen she's disgraced us all, but she's a selfish girl who doesn't know a thing about disgrace, or grace for that matter, either. Still, I take full responsibility for how she's turned out, for who she is. I'm her mother, and I raised her, didn't I? And I failed miserably at it."

Has his mother failed? Luke asks himself. He doesn't know what to use as criteria. The way her three children have turned out? They haven't become drug addicts, or murderers, or thieves, but even if they had, would that be their mother's fault? How could he judge the job she's done parenting them—difficult in the best of circumstances—when he has never been a parent, and knows nothing about it himself? How can anyone be the judge of anyone else's life, when it's impossible to be the judge of one's own? She probably has failed, Luke thinks, but so what? Who hasn't? Who among us looks at his life and sees success?

"Colleen's an adult now," he says. "She knows the difference between right and wrong."

"Ha!" his mother replies. "Colleen is as amoral as a cheetah, or an earthquake, or a fish. Which is why I'm not worried about her, despite the fact that she told me she feels so bad she wants to die. 'Cut the crap,' is what I said to that. Like a cat, she'll always land on her feet, you can bet on it. Frankly, I'm not even worried about her, because I'm sure she'll be able to flirt her way through those pearly gates and win God over, the way she wins over every male within a thirty-mile radius. No, Colleen will be fine. Kate's the one I'm worried about."

It's true that Kate has become fanatical, scouring want-ads, furiously hunting for a new apartment, barely able to stand sleeping in the house where she grew up with Colleen. After removing the hyphen and "Monroe" from her and Audrey's last name, she cashed in the stocks their mother had built up for her over the years, and hired the most high-powered attorney in town, someone who could make sure that Sam wouldn't get visitation rights, much less joint custody, and vowed that he'd never lay eyes on their daughter again. When Sam dropped by their mother's house a few nights ago, Kate stood in the entryway and spoke to him with the steely resolve of one possessed.

"There is nothing to discuss," Luke heard his sister say. "You will never see Audrey again. . . . I'm not punishing her, I'm doing her the supreme favor of allowing her to grow up without knowing a father who's completely lacking in integrity. . . . You have no rights, you threw away your rights when you decided to give in to your perverse desires instead of thinking of the people you supposedly loved most, or at least jumping off a cliff. . . . Oh, yes I can. I can do this, and I will. Watch me."

She shut and locked the door, and then went into the kitchen, where she put on a pot of coffee and read the paper, quietly humming to herself.

Maybe Kate's angry quest for vengeance is extreme, Luke thinks, and yet he admires her tenacity. He thinks about the times he feels the shadow inside him, encroaching, accusing, spreading, of how difficult it is then just to take a shower, go to work, come back home and make himself something to eat, and he has no reason to feel the way he does—he hasn't been betrayed by his crib confidante and his spouse. Whereas Kate: she could tear out her beautiful silky hair, sleep all day, or walk around with eyes red from tearful insomnia. She could take Valium, drink too much, create a cocoon of their mother's house and never want to leave. But instead, she's taking charge of her life.

"Kate will be fine," Luke says.

"She will not be fine. She will never be fine. Everything she's done in her life she's done only to spite me. Going to art school, getting married to a mechanic when she was nineteen . . . this insistence that Audrey never see her father, this ferocious need to move into her own place, these are just the latest examples. She's going to become bitter, if she doesn't watch out, or tough, tough like an overcooked piece of meat nobody can chew. I tried to tell her this, but does she listen to me? That'll be the day."

His mother is right about one thing: That day never comes. Neither does the day when their mother listens to Kate. They talk around each other, through each other—"Lovely weather." "Isn't it?"—like a couple of visiting cousins once removed. Once Kate has found her own apartment, the Friday dinners dwindle to Luke, his mother, and his niece, because now Kate drops Audrey off at the house every Friday afternoon and goes to some artists' co-op to pursue her new interest in pottery, while Sam and Colleen presumably have some tangled romantic dinner of their own. (Chinese takeout? Luke wonders. Taco Bell? Impossible to imagine either of them boiling water, cooking a hard-boiled egg, even owning a pot.) Finally his mother and Kate can't take the polite formalities anymore, and they wage an all-out battle over the fact that Kate isn't allowing Audrey to see Sam, and that their mother feels strongly that this is the biggest mistake, of many mistakes, Kate has made in her entire life.

"What Sam did was abominable, inexcusable," their mother quietly rages, "but Audrey is his daughter, too, and he loves her, and who are you to say she should grow up without experiencing that love?"

"Her mother," is Kate's stony reply. "I'm her mother, and it's none of your goddamn business."

They have come to an impasse; they both glare at Luke, who tries to give them a look back that will say what he's thinking—which is: Don't look at me, I'm just a guy.

He's drowning. He's in the ocean, at night, during a storm. The cold rain is falling on his face, the strong tide tugging him down from below. He's halfway between the shore and a lifeboat—but both are equally, impossibly far away—and his limbs are tired, he can't remember how to swim, and so finally, slowly, he begins to sink.

". . . With the exertions of your hands and feet in the water make the deep, deep sea keep you up." This is a line from *Lord Jim* he often quotes to himself, but now—after he's slept only a few hours two nights in a row—it doesn't help. No matter how hard he tries, he can't stop thinking of the sea as his enemy, the force that's weighing him down, against which his hands and feet won't exert. The shadow is spreading inside him, still squeezing on his lungs, but moving out, gradually expanding, like dirty water, into his arms, his legs, his head, so that he can't lift his arm to answer the phone, can't move his legs to walk to the bathroom, can't lift his head to get up.

This is horrifying, yes, but it's also a problem. He has to call in sick one Wednesday in November because his body aches with a pain he cannot name, and the part-time employee who helps out on weekends and Luke's day off can't sub, so Jerry has to cancel a meeting and drive in from La Ventura. Luke is always afraid that his mother and Kate will notice something's wrong with him when he sees them on Friday afternoons, or when he goes to Kate's new apartment to baby-sit for Audrey, or especially—especially—on Christmas, when he can barely manage to carve the ham, much less sing Yuletide carols at midnight mass.

Fortunately for him, everyone is much too involved in the operatic family crisis to notice the bags under his eyes, or the fifteen pounds he's recently lost, or the fact that he bought all of his presents at the bookstore because he couldn't force himself to go to the mall.

But they will. If things continue like this, eventually they'll notice something's up, and Luke knows—he knows viscerally, with his whole being—that this, above all, must not happen. One morning (he's been up for a week, he looks terrible, awful, a walking zombie) he reaches for the yellow pages and flips to "Psychiatrists." If something isn't wrong with his body, perhaps it's in his mind. He calls the one office listed in San Pablo (who needs a shrink in this beautiful seaside town?), and tells the secretary he has to see a doctor right away.

"Dr. Kim has an opening in three weeks," she says cheerfully.

Luke lets out something that may or may not be a laugh. "I don't think I can wait that long," he says.

"Well, okay, let me see, let me see. . . . Here. Dr. Vernor has a cancellation a week from Wednesday at four-thirty. How does that sound?"

Luke would like to tell her this is an emergency, he needs to see someone today, in ten minutes, right now, but he's the sort who follows the appropriate arrows in bank parking lots even in the middle of the night, who allows women with full carts to go ahead of him at the checkout at Vons, who thanks telemarketers before he hangs up the phone. "You know why civilization is falling to pieces?" his mother always says. "Because nobody gives up their seats to old people anymore. Rudeness isn't a symptom, it's the cause."

"That will be fine," he tells the doctor's secretary.

A week from Wednesday. Ten days. He's waited this long, he can wait ten more days.

Can't he?

Five days before his appointment, his mother tells him that he's going to have to say good-bye to Colleen, as representative of the family. "I just can't bring myself to do it," his mother says.

Kate's divorce came through last week. Justice, logic, and their mother's fierce opinion lost; justice, vengeance, and betrayed single motherhood won: Kate was awarded custody of Audrey; Sam was denied visitation rights; and now that there's nothing to keep them here, Sam and Colleen have decided to go to Phoenix to get married.

Their mother talks with Colleen on the phone a few times a week, but she still hasn't seen her since she heard about the affair. She hands Luke a sack of California oranges, a tin of cashews, and a card-sized envelope marked *Colleen*. "They're leaving early tomorrow," she says.

Luke arrives at their duplex—Kate and Sam's old place—

at seven-thirty the following morning. He's felt all right, almost normal, since he made the appointment, as though just having done that is part of the cure. He gets out of his car as Sam is loading the last boxes into the already full U-Haul attached to his black Mustang, and says, "Good morning."

Sam brushes the hair out of his eyes and squints at Luke. He looks more tired, older, than Luke remembers him from last summer. Sam appears unsure how to behave around an ex- and now soon-to-be brother-in-law, but then he smiles, rather wistfully, and that makes Luke feel they've been through something together. Old friends. Army buddies. Partners in crime. Sam comes forward and warmly shakes his hand.

"Luke. How've ya been?"

"Me? I've been fine. What about you?"

"I'm great. I mean, other than the way the court case turned out, I'm great. You know, I can't say I'm proud of how I got here, but . . ." He gazes toward the duplex. "What can I say? I'm a lucky man."

Luke hands him the oranges and cashews. "These are from Mom, for your trip."

"Sammy?" Colleen yells from the open door, rubbing one tan calf with the other foot. It's early March, still foggy, and chilly, but Colleen has on board shorts and a tank top, and the Converse sneakers she's always used as slippers, her heels pressing down on the backs of the shoes. "Have you seen my driver's license? Hey, Luke."

"It's in the glove compartment."

"Come on in for a minute," she calls to Luke.

He gives Sam a quick nod and walks past him into the duplex.

Colleen's gathering a few stray objects—a hairbrush, a pack of Camels, a bag of Twizzlers—and putting them into a straw bag. The living room is bare and smells of chlorine, cigarette smoke, and limes.

"Mom sent you some food, and a card." Luke hands her the pink envelope, which she immediately rips open.

"A hundred bucks," she says. "Didn't you get a thousand for graduation? And I know Sam and Kate got five when they got married. Well, at least it'll pay for gas. Did I tell you? We've decided not to wait until we get to Phoenix to be married. We're stopping off in Vegas and doing it tomorrow afternoon."

"No, I didn't know," Luke says. "Congratulations. That's great." When Colleen doesn't respond, he adds, "I mean, isn't it?"

Colleen shrugs. "I always wanted a church wedding. You know, with a beautiful white dress, and a priest, and about eight bridesmaids all wearing some hideous shade of mauve. I wanted you to walk me down the aisle. I was going to carry roses, white ones, or maybe the palest, palest pink." She smiles knowingly. "But that's not going to happen. Still, it'll be nice to arrive as husband and wife. Nobody there will . . . well, you know. They'll think we're just like any other married couple. You should come out and see us in Phoenix. We're going to buy a house with a pool."

Phoenix. Luke thinks of retirees, and asthmatics, and religious fanatics who wander into the desert, praying, sweating, dropping cyanide.

"I know what you're thinking," she says. "You're thinking I won't make a very good wife."

"I wasn—"

"But I will! I've been faithful to Sam for almost a year now, and monogamy isn't nearly as hard as I thought it would be. I've been learning how to cook, and I'm thinking of having a little garden, well, maybe only a cactus garden to start out with, but desert plants are really beautiful once you get used to them. Sam wants to have kids—not now, but someday—which, I mean, okay, it's a little scary, but I think it's probably a good idea. I mean, how else is he supposed to get over not being able to see Audrey anymore?"

Underneath her apparent happiness and pride over her nine-month monogamy, Luke senses a thin tremor of hysteria, and thinks he sees the shadow of some new lover, some other Sam, some distraction and pastime, some flirtation gone too far, looming somewhere in the future.

"I'm glad," he tells her. "I'm glad."

She walks over and hugs him tightly, and when she breaks away, there are tears in her eyes. "I'm going to miss you, big brother," she says. She picks up her bag and a can of Diet Coke, and they walk outside together. Sam is inside the running Mustang, looking at a map. Colleen turns to Luke one last time, and in her bright blue eyes he sees fear.

"Have you ever seen a photograph of Mars?" she whispers hoarsely. "That's what Arizona looks like." She pushes back her hair and stares at the U-Haul. "What the fuck am I doing?" she says, and it occurs to Luke that she might be driving off into the sunset with Sam not because she wants to, because she loves him, but as a kind of penance. He wouldn't put it past the quirky perambulations of Colleen's mind to believe that marrying Sam and buying a house with a pool—the white picket fence of the Southwest—would be a just punishment for having stolen him from Kate in the first place. Like Cain's, Colleen's sentence will be exile, and for an instant, as she stares at the bucking bronco on the side of the U-Haul, she looks as though she fears it worse than death.

But then she nods, as if answering her own question, remembering what the fuck it is she's doing. "Tell Mom I'll call her tonight. I'm not allowed to drop by," she adds smiling. "Tell Kate I love her. Kiss Audrey for me. Good-bye, Brother Luke, don't forget to visit!"

She takes off down the walkway, an exuberant teenager headed for the beach, and gets inside the loaded-down car.

Luke is in the waiting room of Dr. Vernor's office. The decor is spa-peaceful, Zen-like, with contemporary white chairs, a low teak table topped with a bonsai plant, a Japanese print of two figures in the rain on the eggshell wall. He could be in some rich person's clean living room, or the lounge of a tasteful hotel, or perhaps the lobby of a holistic health center, waiting for a massage—that is, if he weren't so damned scared. The only thing that might give away the room's identity is the eclecticism of the magazines nestled in the gunmetal-gray rack: *Art & Antiques, Seventeen, Field & Stream, Harper's, Newsweek, Sports Illustrated,*

Psychology Today, together proclaiming: Look, all kinds of people need to see shrinks.

The woman across from him—the only other person in the waiting room—is blithely reading a book by Lee Iacocca. She's wearing a smart navy suit with pearls and pumps; her big hair's coiffed and sprayed; her makeup is tasteful and perfectly applied: Luke wonders why in the world this together, successful businesswoman is here. When she reaches to turn a page, her jacket sleeve edges down her arm, and Luke sees the white bandage around her wrist. He doesn't realize he's staring, until she glances up from her book, meets his eyes, and gives him a look that says, "Yeah? So? You've never considered it before?" and Luke, caught, looks away.

He gazes through the second-story window at the cerulean sky and considers what he'll tell the doctor. He's been doing this on and off for the past ten days—rehearsing his spiel in his head—and he wants to go over it once more before he has to say the irrevocable words aloud.

He's been experiencing some peculiar symptoms. Chronic insomnia, weight loss, general fatigue. An amorphous ache throughout his body that he thought might be physical, but he went to the clinic and they could find nothing wrong. This began, he'll tell the doctor, when he was a child, and he'll proceed to narrate everything, from his father's death to the shadow that materialized in front of his eyes under the avocado tree at his mom's. This shadow, he'll explain, hasn't really left him. It's spreading out, squeezing on his lungs, weighing down his limbs, taking up more and more space, like some metastasizing malignant tumor. It hasn't yet reached his hands and feet, but that's just a matter of time. He's convinced—he knows (*I know*, he'll emphasize to the doctor)—that when it does, when it spreads to every cell, through every artery, when it reaches every inch of his body, he'll be dead.

"Luke?" the receptionist calls. "Dr. Vernor is ready to see you now."

Luke stands. He glances one last time at the bandaged businesswoman, who gives him a ghastly smirk: she knows what's in store for him even if he doesn't.

He walks to the open door.

Haunted

Grief was a blooming flower in the mouth. It was a gardenia: white, redolent, untouchable. She could feel it blossoming even now, taking up roots in her lungs, immersing her tongue in its perfumed, sickly-sweet taste.

Air, Kate thought. She needed some fresh air to remove the floral taste of grief. She sat up and looked around her old bedroom, trying to see by only the digital clock—its glowing green numbers a menacing reminder that she had been trying to sleep, without success, for the past two hours—until she found what she'd been searching for: a sweatshirt. She pulled it over her head and stepped into her clogs, then went down the stairs, through the kitchen, out the back door, and into the dark outside.

Kate didn't believe in anything she couldn't see with her own eyes, touch with her own hands. When she was a little girl, the stories about Jesus' empty tomb and Noah's ark had never seemed any more real to her than the ones about Hansel and Gretel or Goldilocks and the Three Bears. Later, in art school, even painting had been too abstract for her, too emotional; she'd preferred to sink her hands into moist, cool earth, to create something that she could pick up, run her fingers over, touch, fondle, smell. She certainly didn't believe in heaven, in some patriarchal God and harp-playing cherubs floating on a silvery-pink cloud; when you died, you died, ashes to ashes, dust to dust—and Luke was dead.

Then why, when she stepped onto the back deck of her mother's house, did she feel him there, really feel him, the way you know without looking that someone is staring at you?

"Luke?" she said aloud. It felt as if he was tugging on something inside her, the way Audrey used to tug on her pants leg whenever she'd urgently wanted her to come see. "Luke? What is it? Is that you?"

Maybe, it occurred to her, she was losing her mind.

She went back inside, shaken, and into the bathroom, where she swallowed some NyQuil to help her fall asleep.

Where was Audrey? Her bed was empty, the comforter in a heap, her mismatched pajamas on the floor, her running shoes tossed inside the open closet. Kate checked the bathroom, then went back downstairs into the kitchen, where she'd put on a pot of coffee minutes before, and found her sitting in the breakfast nook.

"Hey, honey. Where were you?"

"Nowhere. Just outside."

"Did you go for a run?"

"Nope."

"Oh. I couldn't find you. You're up kind of early, aren't you?"

"It's after seven."

Kate looked at her, searching for signs of insomnia and tears, but found only a carapace—opaque, hard, unreadable—covering whatever was going on inside.

"How'd you sleep?" she asked gently, because it was the closest she could get to asking, "How are you?"

Audrey was noncommittal. "Fine."

Kate poured herself a glass of water and stared into the backyard, remembering when she and Luke and Colleen had made a village by tying sheets from the rubber tree all the way to the pine against the back fence. She wasn't aware that she was crying until she tasted a salty tear. Why? Why in the world had he done it?

She thought she could see Luke against the counter, licking an ice cream cone, peering at it intently through his wire-rimmed glasses, a napkin politely placed between his hand and the brown cone. Pistachio. He had always ordered pistachio.

Kate wiped her tears. "I just can't believe he's dead."

When Audrey didn't say anything, she turned toward the breakfast nook. It was empty. Audrey was gone.

Kate's mother came into the kitchen at eight-thirty. She was wearing a fuzzy blue bathrobe and the slippers shaped like monkey faces that Audrey had given her last Christmas as a joke; her mom claimed they were the warmest slippers she'd ever had, and wore them all the time. Her face was sallow, her eyes adamantine stones, and Kate tried to imagine what she'd thought or felt when she'd put those grinning monkeys onto her feet this morning. Perhaps she hadn't even looked at them.

"Hello," Kate said. She was sitting at the table, drinking her sixth cup of coffee, which was creating an acidic burning in her stomach that she rather liked. "That's a fresh pot, if you want some coffee."

Her mother looked at her with an expression of bewilderment, as if thinking, Coffee? or perhaps, Who are you?

Her mother's mind and body seemed to be shutting down to their essentials, and things like language and nourishment had gone the way of diamond earrings and brocade scarves. Kate wondered if she should call a doctor, but knew there was no point. There was no cure for what her mother had.

"Are you ready?" Alek asked. He had come over at nine with doughnuts and orange juice, and although she hadn't been hungry, Kate had eaten two whole-wheat doughnuts, one jelly-filled glazed, and a chocolate-cream eclair. Now it was a quarter to ten, and she was feeling sick.

"As I'll ever be," she said.

"This one." Kate pointed to the plainest, cheapest coffin there was—after seeing coffins made of teak, cherry, oak, bronze, even a gold-plated one lined with white satin fit for Elvis that cost more than she'd paid for their condo—knowing that Luke wouldn't have wanted anything elaborate or expensive.

"I should tell you," the funeral director said, in a lowered, confidential tone, "we cannot guarantee that worms won't get into that one."

Kate let out a quick laugh. "Worms," she repeated. "Maybe I didn't make this clear. My brother is dead. He committed suicide. He doesn't care about worms."

Back in their childhood home, Luke was waiting for her. He was in the kitchen, helping himself to a beer. He was in the family room, sitting on the couch beside Audrey, who was channel-surfing through a whirl of gyrating teenagers and polar bears and car commercials, all of which Luke gazed upon with the fascinated incomprehension of a traveler from another galaxy. He was there when Alek brought in the cat, when Audrey held Rosie to her chest; he smiled faintly as Audrey buried her face in the Manx's soft fur and cooed reassuringly into her pointed ear. He was listening when she phoned their mother's favorite priest, Father Francis, who agreed to perform a graveside service after mass on Sunday; when Father Francis came to the house an hour later and their mother refused to see him, Luke guiltily hung his head. He was the silence she heard every time she wondered why, every time she asked herself how he could have done this to their mother, every time she searched her brain to try to figure out what he'd been thinking when he'd written that will, swallowed those pills, downed that bottle of wine. He was in the backyard, mowing the grass. Kate saw him—imagined him—there, while she was loading the dishwasher.

"Oh my God. The grass. Look at how long it is. How did it get so long, after only a week? We need to mow it for the reception tomorrow."

"I'll take care of it," Alek told her from his seat at the table. "Want me to mow it right now?"

"I don't know. Won't it be getting dark soon? Should you wait until morning?"

"It'll be harder to mow then because of the dew. Audrey?" he called.

"What," Audrey said from the family room.

"Come here a minute, will you?"

Audrey slowly sauntered toward them, and stood in the archway between the family room and the kitchen. "Yeah?"

"I'm going to mow the lawn. Will you come with me and rake up the grass?"

Audrey looked at her mother. "Do I have to?"

"Yes, you have to," Kate said. "It won't take long."

Kate watched from the kitchen as they came out of the detached garage, Alek pushing the mower, Audrey dragging the plastic trashcan for green waste. Alek pulled the cord, once, twice, three times, until it caught; a few moments later, her mother suddenly appeared in the backyard, waving her arms. Kate hurried out the back door.

"Turn that thing off," her mother shouted. They were the first words Kate had heard her speak since she'd learned of Luke's death, and her voice was damaged and raw.

Alek immediately complied.

"Mom, are you all right?" Kate approached her and touched her arm.

Her mother shook her away. "Put this damn mower back where you found it, right now. Audrey? You can get rid of that garbage can. Nobody's mowing this lawn. Do you hear me? Nobody."

Alek looked shocked, but he managed to nod. "All right," he said. "I'll go put it back."

"Wait," Kate told Alek, then turned to her mother: "People are coming here tomorrow. For the reception. Don't you think—"

"I think that all of you are guests in my house. And if you want to continue to stay here, you'll do as I tell you."

Kate, Alek, and Audrey looked at one another. Finally Alek said, "You heard your grandma. Let's go put this stuff away."

When Kate went upstairs to kiss Audrey good night, she found her lying in bed stroking Rosie, who sat like a sphinx beside her knees. With her freckles and smooth skin and messy hair framing her face, Audrey looked so innocent and young. Kate felt an animal surge of protectiveness. She wanted to protect her daughter not from predators, not from danger, just from pain. This pain. Whatever she was feeling, right now.

"I guess your uncle had good instincts leaving Rosie to you," Kate said. "She sure seems to take to you, doesn't she?"

Audrey was silent, and Kate sat down beside her. "You

know, when I was your age, I thought my mother had all the answers. I thought being an adult meant that you were sure about, well, everything. Your grandma lost her husband when she was the age I am now, and she seemed ancient to me back then, but just wait until you're thirty-three, you'll see it doesn't feel so ancient."

"I don't think you have all the answers, Mom."

"Well, good. Because I don't." Kate sighed. "All this is to say that I want to help you, but I'm not sure how. I don't know why your uncle killed himself, but I know he loved you, Audrey."

Audrey gave her a weird smile—twisted and wise—and Kate felt her face become warm. The truth was, she didn't know that Luke had loved Audrey, and even if he had, as Audrey would say, so what?

"Mom?"

"Yeah?"

"Is your sister coming to the funeral tomorrow?"

Kate tried not to show her surprise. "Yes. Why?"

"I was just wondering." Audrey closed her eyes. "I'm tired now. I want to go to sleep."

She rubbed her closed lids, and Kate had an image of her newborn daughter's fingers: delicate, fragile, little pink worms with tiny nails—a miracle.

"Audrey . . ."

"What?"

I'm sorry, were the words that had been on Kate's tongue, but they made no sense. What apology had she wanted to make? Luke was the one who had killed himself. Luke was the one who had brought them to this tension, these silences, to wherever they were now, to wherever they'd be going.

"Nothing," Kate said, and switched off the bedside light.

"You are the strongest person I know," Alek had told her when they'd stood in the driveway and said good night, but now, alone in the dark in the room she'd shared with Colleen for more than half her life, she knew: She wasn't strong, she was weak, she had failed. She remembered when Luke hadn't let her go skateboarding with him and Tommy Lanz, and she'd called him ugly. "I don't really want to go skateboarding with you," she'd shouted, "you ugly, ugly Luke!" And the look on his face: wounded, accepting, as though he knew she was telling him the truth, and didn't blame her for it in the least. "I didn't mean it," she'd immediately added, and she hadn't—it was the kind of meaningless insult she and Colleen exchanged every day of the week—but it was too late. The damage had been done.

"You weren't ugly, you were beautiful," Kate whispered into the dark.

And she could feel him there, listening, not believing her, even now.

A strange sensation, remembering, upon awakening, that today is the day you will bury your brother, a sinking pit the color of a blue-black crow's wing, the same slick, unguent shine. Kate wanted the day to be over, yet she was almost looking forward to the hours ahead as well, in the same way she'd prefer to die conscious rather than in her sleep. It was her destiny, her fate, and no matter how painful it might be, she wanted to meet it: to attend her brother's funeral; watch his coffin swallowed into the ground; after ten years, see Colleen.

The black limousine pulled into the drive at ten-thirty. The service would begin in an hour. Kate had been pacing, waiting for Colleen to show up, all morning.

"It's just like her to do this," she told Alek.

"Maybe she's going to meet us at the cemetery."

"Why hasn't she called? Should we wait?"

Alek glanced at his watch. He was wearing a charcoal jacket Kate had always liked, but now everything about him mildly irritated her, and she hated the way it fit across the chest, hated the leather buttons on the sleeves, hated how it clashed with his conservative navy blue tie.

"Let's give her ten more minutes. I'll go talk to the driver."

Why did he have to be so practical, so calm? Kate imagined a nuclear explosion, everyone running around like ants trying to escape a descending hand, while Alek methodically searched for bottled water, canned goods, an airtight sealed room. She had an urge to slap his face.

"I love you," he said, brushing her cheek with the back of his fingers. "I don't know if it helps for you to be reminded of that now, but I do."

His gaze was her admonishment. She was mean, petty. Unlovable. What would she do if he weren't here, a solid rock unwracked by grief?

"Yes," she said, bringing his fingers to her lips and kissing them. "Yes, of course it helps."

Colleen didn't show. They rode in the solemn, air-conditioned limo without her to the cemetery, where they were ushered into the private waiting room for families. Kate leaned back in the chintz-covered armchair and shut her tired eyes. When she opened them again, Colleen was standing in the doorway. Kate's heart skipped a beat, then pounded rapidly to make up for the loss. Her sister had faint creases on either side of her mouth and white lines in the otherwise tanned skin around her eyes; her face was more formed, more adult, than it had been ten years before—and yet she looked the same. Her hair was still long, wavy, the color of wheat; she still emitted an aura of confidence and energy, the way people do who get whatever they want. She was wearing a navy-and-white floral print dress and white leather mules, which should have looked inappropriate, but did not. She went directly to their mother and crouched, putting her arms around her, kissing her on the cheek.

"I'm sorry," she said, in her rushed, low voice, the sound the wind would make if it could speak. "I had an accident in Bakersfield last night, I had to rent a car this morning. Mom, I love you, I'm sorry."

Her mother patted Colleen's arm with the distracted air of a saint listening to someone rave about something insignificant and worldly, a ketchup stain on a blouse, and after a few long seconds, Colleen straightened.

Kate had been imagining their meeting for the past two days, for the past ten years, and wondered, even as late as this morning, whether she would feel rage. But now that it was happening—now that she was staring into her sister's ocean-blue eyes, which were gazing back at her without embarrassment or guilt or even apology but in simple purblind grief, now that their brother's body was in a cheap pine coffin in the adjoining room, and their brother himself gone—Kate found that she felt a wave of comfort at the sight of her sister's sorrowful face, the face of a woman who has lost her brother, a mirror, Kate imagined, of her own. She stepped forward and hugged Colleen, hard. "I've missed you," she managed to whisper.

Colleen curled her head into Kate's neck, the weight of it there comfortingly familiar to Kate, as though it had never been gone.

"I missed you too."

The way the six men struggled to carry Luke's coffin from the hearse uphill to the grave. The sight of it resting on the red plastic pulleys, then disappearing into the open earth.

The sound of ducks quacking at the bottom of the hill, two children tossing them bread.

The scent of flowers. Roses, lilies, carnations, a bunch of wild lupine and orange poppies plucked by Colleen from the side of the road: a saccharine scent masking the scent of death, perfume covering the pungent odor of unwashed skin.

A few rows away, a man spritzing a black headstone with a spray bottle, wiping it with chamois cloth, then spritzing again, in a Sisyphean effort to make the marble shine as brightly as his grief.

The mourners standing across from where the family was sitting: Luke's boss and his wife, Luke's landlord, Kate's friend Keisha. The shock of the paltry cortege, not the knowledge of it—for who else would have come?—but the sight of it, the fact that it was only these few people who had come to care for Luke in his thirty-six years on the planet.

Audrey picking at a thread of her black skirt, sneaking glances at Colleen.

The sound of the priest's baritone: "In the name of the Father, the Son, the Holy Spirit, Amen."

Her mother crossing herself slowly, so slowly, not sure exactly where her forehead, chest, and shoulders were located.

"The Lord is my Shepherd; I shalt not want. . . ."

But it was another passage from the Bible that came into Kate's mind, and wouldn't leave.

Am I my brother's keeper?

Kate brewed coffee and decaf and set out a little silver pitcher of cream and a bowl of sugar. She served tea sandwiches and cold cuts. She said, "Thank you," when anyone said, "I'm sorry," and, "You can't blame yourself, Jerry," to Luke's boss, when he said he should have given Luke more vacation time and better health insurance. When she had finished performing every hostess duty she could think of for the gathering of nine people (including Father Francis, and excluding her mother, who was upstairs in her room), she stood in the kitchen to catch her breath. Luke was sitting in the breakfast nook, a sheepish expression on his face, as if he hadn't meant to put her to so much trouble.

Forty-five minutes after they'd arrived, the guests began to leave. At the door, Keisha told Kate, "I just want you to know, we can reschedule the opening, so don't worry about finishing your stuff in time for December. We can do it in the spring. Or whenever." As she spoke, Kate felt as though she had amnesia, and were being summoned with a snatch of her old life. She had been a ceramist. She had rendered myths into clay. She'd been obsessed with the form of a pot. With the color of a glaze. With the expression of a Greek goddess, a Cherokee hero, a horse, a spider, a cow.

"All right," Kate said. "I won't worry."

Keisha hugged her. "Bye, honey. I'm sorry for your loss. I just want you to know, I think you're doing great."

Kate watched her walk down the drive, then shut the door. "This is great?" she said to Alek. "What's so great about it?"

"Great is functioning. Making coffee. Setting out food. Staying in the race. That's all."

Kate couldn't help thinking the criteria had gotten very low. She pinched the inner corners of her eyes. Alek said, "Hey," and wrapped his arms around her, and kissed the top of her head. But it wasn't Alek she wanted. She broke away and walked toward the kitchen and Colleen.

"You don't have to do that," Kate told her sister, who was rinsing the dirty plates before loading them into the dishwasher.

"Look, you organized this whole thing, the least I can do is these few dishes."

"No, I mean you don't have to rinse them off first."

"Oh."

"You know Mom and her electrical appliances. This one could clean the pan she baked lasagne in a month ago, no problem."

Alek came into the kitchen with a tray of coffee cups. "I'll take care of the rest," he said. "Why don't you two go sit down?"

Colleen glanced at him, then at Kate. "Is he for real?"

Kate smiled. "Yes."

Colleen set down her dishrag and turned off the water. "All right," she said. "You got a deal."

Kate followed her into the family room, where they sat on opposite ends of the couch. Music poured in faintly from above: Audrey was upstairs in her room.

"Who would have guessed," Colleen said. "Mom owns a leather couch."

Kate stared at her, trying not to be obvious, but Colleen said, "What? Do I have chocolate all over my face?"

"You and Luke. You have the same mouth. I guess I never noticed before."

Colleen fidgeted, tapping her fingers together.

"I'm sorry," Kate said. "Does mentioning Luke make you nervous?"

"What? Oh, you mean this." She inspected her hands, then put them on her lap. "I quit smoking when I got pregnant with Jen. I know it's terrible to say, but I didn't want to. Sam made me. Sam and my doctor. It's been over seven years, and I still can't figure out what to do with my hands. Jingling keys helps. But my keys are in my purse, which is God knows where."

She showed no embarrassment, no self-consciousness, at the mention of Sam's name, and Kate didn't feel any herself. They might have been talking about some friendly acquaintance they had known through school, instead of the father of their three children, the man Kate had once loved, and Colleen still did love.

"How is Sam?"

"Okay. Kind of tired, actually. He works long hours at the garage, but you know, you have to, when you own your own business. He tried to take up golf to relax," Colleen said, "but he was awful at it."

Kate pictured Sam in white slacks and a lavender shirt, and it made her smile. "I'll bet," she said, and immediately stopped smiling, because she remembered Luke was dead.

"Jennifer's the one who plays. She's the athlete in our family. Kind of like Audrey, I guess."

"And Ryan?"

"Ry likes to draw. Takes after his aunt Kate, I tell him."

Aunt Kate. She was Aunt Kate to two children she'd never met, never seen. It was ridiculous.

"Luke kept me up on your career," Colleen said, a hint of shyness in her voice. "I'm really happy for you. I always knew you'd be a success."

"I don't feel like much of a success right now."

Colleen didn't say anything for a moment, and then she

leaned forward. "Luke was depressed. There was nothing we could have done about that, any of us. It was his life, his choice. He refused to get help."

"Refused? What do you mean, refused? Did you know he was depressed? I mean, while he was alive?"

Colleen rested her chin on her knees, hugging her tan calves with her even tanner arms. "Right after New Year's," she said, "Luke called me at work and told me he couldn't get out of bed. He tried to laugh it off, you know, but there was something about his voice. . . . I canceled my appointments and drove to the airport, without even packing a bag.

"I had to get José to open the door for me, because it was locked. But everything seemed fine. The place was real neat, you know. But when I went into the bedroom . . . Kate, it was a disaster. Empty pizza cartons, glasses, dirty laundry, books all over the floor, it was like the day after some totally wild party. And there was Luke, pale, with beard stubble—I'd never seen him unshaven before—and he literally could not get out of bed."

Kate didn't understand. Luke? Who never got sick, never missed a day of work, whose apartment was always so tidy? When was the last time she'd been in his bedroom? When Audrey had been five? Six? She lived less than two miles away. Why hadn't he called her? Why hadn't she known?

"I helped him into the bathroom, and then into the living room," Colleen went on, "and I made him sit on the couch and tell me what the hell was happening, but he said he didn't know, he just felt down about the new year, and he didn't think he could go to work, and he was just in the doldrums, he supposed. And I was like, This is not the doldrums, okay? I told him about a girl I knew who used to be a total basket case but who was on Prozac now and totally fine, but he just smiled and said that it was life and you couldn't really medicate life and, anyway, he was feeling better already. So I drove him to work and cleaned his room and picked him up, and we went out to dinner and he really did seem much better, and the next day he said, 'Okay, you can leave now, I'm fine.' I told him I thought he should see someone, you know, a shrink, but he said that it was just the New Year's blues combined with a hangover because he'd gotten a little toasted, and I believed him. I mean, by the time I left, he really did seem fine."

"Did you ever tell Mom?"

"He made me promise not to. He said she'd overreact." Colleen let out a short, bitter laugh. "As it turns out, that would have been impossible."

"Why didn't he tell me?"

"Come on."

"What do you mean? I could have checked up on him, I could have—"

"Because. Nobody wants to tell their perfect sister to come on over so she can see them lying in bed beside some empty pizza boxes and a pool of vomit. He looked up to you, Kate. He wouldn't have wanted you to see him like that."

"I didn't know," Kate said. "I was so . . . If only I'd known."

"I spent a lot of time thinking about this in the car," Colleen said carefully. "And the way I look at it, suicide must have seemed like some kind of a solution to Luke. I mean, it may not make sense to us, but it must have made sense to him. That's why I don't—that's why I try not to feel guilty. He wouldn't have wanted that. Just the idea of it would have perplexed him. It was his solution to his problems, and I don't think they had anything to do with us. It's almost . . . egotistical of us to feel guilty."

"If only . . ." Kate said, but she couldn't go on.

"See, that's what I mean. You can drive yourself crazy with that. If only I'd called him Thursday night. If only I'd given him this beautiful Waterman pen as soon as I bought it instead of waiting for Christmas. If only I'd taken him to the Grand Canyon when he came to visit. You can go on and on."

If only, Kate was still thinking. If only I had been the kind of sister who'd made him want to stay alive.

Kate looked into the mirror above the bathroom sink. Her eyes were swollen, her skin aniline blue. She was getting a pimple on her chin. Her cheeks seemed rounder than usual; she had been eating compulsively, without appetite, for two days. She touched her smooth, shoulder-length hair, and suddenly was overwhelmed by the sensation that this was not who she was. The image in front of her was just skin over bones, with wide lips, hazel eyes, reddish hair—but what was skin? what were bones? She ran her forefinger down the length of her jaw, from her ear to her chin, then to the other ear, feeling the skeleton below. "This isn't me," she whispered, though she really had no idea what she meant.

And then she saw Luke. He was in her archless brows, in

the almond shape of her eyes, in the square ridge of her forehead. He was there, in the mirror, in her face. Their face. She quickly turned off the lights and stood in the almost-pitch dark, afraid.

"Damn you," she whispered, but without conviction, with a softness, in fact, as though what she was really saying was something entirely different, as though she was saying, "I love you." Which was something she'd never said to him when he'd been alive.

The next morning, Kate was pouring herself a glass of water when she saw Colleen and Audrey sitting in patio chairs on the back deck. Their manes of wavy hair were pulled back into matching ponytails, fastened with velvet scrunchies. The two of them together was a sight Kate would have done anything—had done anything—to avoid ten years before, and now that it was happening, it seemed a combination of natural (why shouldn't Audrey be sitting outside with her aunt?) and unsettling (what were they talking about?). Their heads were bent toward each other conspiratorially.

Kate watched, transfixed, as Colleen smoothed one of Audrey's eyebrows, her finger gently running its length, a gesture so intimate it shocked her. She didn't feel jealous so much as confused: How long had they been sitting out there? When had they gotten to know each other so well? Why was Audrey smiling shyly instead of pulling her head away? And what day was it, anyway? Monday, after nine. Shouldn't Audrey be in school?

"Morning," she said, stepping onto the deck.

"Oh, Kate, you and Audrey are going to have to come visit us in Phoenix. Jenny and Ry would just love to meet their cousin."

Kate looked at Audrey, who looked away. "Audrey, you're late for school. How come you didn't get me up?"

"Aunt Colleen said she'd give me a ride."

"You've already missed first period."

"Geometry with Mr. Monotone. She told me. God, I can't believe the man's still teaching there. He must be a hundred by now." Colleen grabbed her bag and stood up.

"I can drive Audrey," Kate said. "It'll just take me a minute to—"

"Mom, we're leaving right now."

"I have some errands to run anyway," Colleen said. "And besides. This'll give me and Audrey a chance to say good-bye."

Later that morning, Colleen and Kate sat at the kitchen table sipping coffee. "You know what I keep thinking about?" Colleen asked. "The time Luke got Mrs. Longman's cat down from that tree. Remember?"

"Vaguely," Kate said.

"Don't you remember? Mrs. Longman had that Persian she never let outside, and then one day it got out and the Darbys' dog chased it, and it ran into the Darbys' eucalyptus. Mrs. Longman was just about to call the fire department, but Luke said he'd climb up. The cat kept going higher and higher, and so did Luke, and we were totally scared, because we thought he was going to fall, but he picked it up and brought it down. There were scratches all over his arms and face."

"Luke was a good boy." The voice, rough with lack of use, was their mother's. Kate turned and saw her standing in the doorway.

Colleen looked up at her and smiled, dreamy, close-lipped. "Yes, he was, wasn't he?"

Colleen was driving Luke's red Toyota to Phoenix. She'd returned the rental car, and was planning on driving with Sam from Phoenix to Bakersfield to pick up her Jeep sometime later, although she hadn't told Sam.

"Will he mind?" Kate had asked.

"Dunno. But even if he does, he'll do it." Was this a clue to their marriage, Kate had wondered. When she had been married to Sam, it had been she who would have done something—anything—for him, not the other way around.

Kate stood on the front porch, waiting while Colleen said good-bye to their mother in private. She was studying the grass. It looked as if it hadn't been mowed in months. It was mangy, unkempt, some patches taller than others, some strands yellow, some green. Should she water it? If she turned on the sprinklers, wouldn't it just grow longer? If she didn't, wouldn't it turn yellowish brown?

Colleen walked outside with her overnight bag. She had on jeans and a V-neck sweater that revealed her cleavage, and Kate remembered with some amusement that she had spent many years being jealous of her sister's more ample breasts.

"Tell Alek I said good-bye."

"Sure you don't want to spend another night?"

"I've got to get back home. You know. Sam, the kids, work. Not to mention the dog, who probably hasn't been walked since Saturday morning."

Kate smiled. Colleen had turned into a wife, a mother, a dog-walker, a nonsmoker, a real estate agent, and oddly, it didn't even seem that odd.

She tossed her bag on the backseat, got into the car, and leaned toward the passenger side.

"Hey."

"Yeah?"

"Saturday night, when I had that accident? I woke up into the divider, into the airbag and everything, and I thought, I can't believe I'm going to die before I see Kate again. Before I talk to her, or hear her voice, or even know what she looks like anymore. Those were my dying thoughts. It was only later that I realized how strange it would be to die on the way to Luke's funeral. Except I didn't die. I was totally fine."

Before Kate could think of how to respond, Colleen was backing out of the drive and speeding away.

Kate was chopping vegetables for a stir-fry when she looked up to see Audrey in the breakfast nook, sipping a glass of juice. This had happened a lot these past few days: like a cat, silent and graceful, Audrey slunk around, rarely making her presence felt. Like a cat, Kate thought, or a ghost.

"Did you have a nice time with your aunt?"

"It was all right."

"Just all right? Colleen said she really enjoyed meeting you."

Audrey shrugged.

"I know the situation's a little awkward," Kate said, choosing her words with care, "and I understand that your feelings about her might be complicated, but—"

"Why do you have to make such a big deal out of everything?"

"I'm not making a big—"

"We talked for a few minutes out on the patio, and then she gave me a ride to school. It was no big deal, Mom. Really."

"All I asked was whether or not you had a nice time."

"We had a fabulous time. It was simply mahvelous. It was the best ride to school I've ever had. Is that what you want to hear? Or no. Maybe you want to hear, 'Omigod it was like, totally awful. Your sister is such a total ditz.' "

"Audrey . . ." Was she about to cry? Kate reached out to touch her hand, but Audrey pulled it away.

"I'm gonna go check on Grandma," Audrey said, and walked out of the room.

Should she go after her? Force her to talk about what she was going through? Or maybe just give her a hug and let her know that it was all right, she didn't need to talk if she didn't want to? There should have been instructions. A VCR came with instructions, a portable phone, even a vacuum cleaner. Why shouldn't a child? Kate was confused, and her confusion made her afraid.

She picked up her knife and went back to slicing cabbage, concentrating on its pale green color, the smooth vellum skin below her hand.

Three days after the funeral, it rained from morning until night. Kate awakened to the sad, comforting sound, spent the day listening to its steady rhythm, and fell asleep as the lullaby turned into a storm. The next morning, when she went outside to retrieve the paper, it seemed to her that the grass had grown another inch. The young cat from next door was playing in it, catching moths and attacking long weeds. She reached down for the newspaper, swathed in plastic, and heard:

"Kate! Excuse me, Kate!"

It was Mrs. Chen, who lived two houses down, standing on the sidewalk. She was wearing a pantsuit and carrying a bag embossed with interlocking C's.

"Yes?"

"Listen, my boy, Bob, he mow your mother lawn free. No charge ten bucks, like usual. I tell him, it's least you can do for Miss Flannigan, after she lose only son. He over today after school, you want."

Bob Chen, who was twelve, and wore baggy shorts and Porno for Pyros T-shirts, was as American as egg rolls and pizza. A budding entrepreneur, he mowed half the lawns on the block, charging extra for cleaning gutters and raking leaves.

"That's kind of you and Bob," Kate said, "but it isn't that. My daughter and I can do it. It's just . . . My mother isn't quite ready yet. To have the lawn mowed."

"Not quite ready yet?" Mrs. Chen repeated, perhaps unsure of the meaning of these simple words.

Kate sighed. "You know. It was Luke, my brother, who always mowed the lawn."

"Ah," Mrs. Chen said. "She wait for him come back. I understand."

Kate was relieved it made sense to someone.

"Listen, when she ready he no come back, you call Bob. He do good job. First time free. Okay?"

With that, she walked down the street, past her perfectly groomed lawn with its flourishing rose garden, and got into her black BMW. Kate turned around. It had been two weeks, and the grass was as high as the portulaca beside the California palm.

"What am I supposed to do? She won't talk to me."

Kate and Alek were having a postprandial cup of coffee on the deck. Audrey was upstairs doing homework; Kate's mother had already gone to bed. The backyard was quiet and dark, lit only by the moon.

"You have to give her time. Maybe this is how she's dealing with her uncle's suicide. By pulling away from you."

"Yeah, but do you think that's healthy?"

"I don't know. She seemed fine to me when I gave her a

ride home. I mean, she talked about her classes and everything. Maybe you two need to spend some time alone together."

The idea made Kate panic. Audrey was so angry with her, so sullen, Kate couldn't imagine spending more than a few minutes alone with her anymore. But maybe that was why they needed to do just that.

"You're probably right. We should do something this weekend. Go on a picnic or something. Alek?"

"Hmm?"

"What if it's more than that? What if she's really not . . . okay?"

Alek reached for her hand. "Audrey is level-headed, and tough. She'll be fine." When Kate didn't say anything, Alek asked, "What are you afraid of?"

"I'm afraid that I won't know if something's really wrong with Audrey, just like I didn't know something was really wrong with Luke."

"You're not afraid she'd kill herself?"

"I'm afraid she'd really need something from me and I wouldn't know."

Alek let out a deep breath. "How's this for a truism? We can't know what other people need or feel unless they tell us."

"What if she won't tell me?"

"That's her choice."

Everything was letting go. Kate imagined all the people she loved as helium balloons, sailing into the air, while she stood with her feet planted on the ground, watching them become smaller and smaller.

The middle of the night. She awakened to hear one word: "Kate." Clear and unmistakable. Her brother's voice, the liquid-gold texture of rum.

Kate didn't like to leave the house, which was warm and fuzzy with grief and dense with the dust of Luke's memory. Whenever she did venture outside, she felt she was lacking something, much the way she used to feel when Audrey was a baby and she left her with Sam or her mom. And yet she knew she had to go home, get back to work, return to normal life. She knew this. But every morning after she dropped off Audrey at school, she ended up driving back to her mom's.

One morning she forced herself to go home. She scooped up the newspapers on the porch and the mail overflowing from the box, set them on the kitchen counter without looking at them, and went into her studio. The sight startled her. After she'd gotten off the phone with Mr. Hernandez, she hadn't bothered to clean her tools, wipe the tables, sweep the floor—she'd simply covered her sculpture and left—and now there was dried clay everywhere, each speck of it a reminder that Luke was dead.

She sat down at her table, grasped a corner of the oilcloth covering the larger-than-life-sized head, and slowly lifted it away. It was like looking into a three-dimensional clay mirror, and the irony of having so acutely rendered the features that now seemed so random and meaningless struck her as a darkly karmic joke. The face stared back at her with what was supposed to have been . . . what? fear? hope? love? but at the moment seemed blankness. Or maybe confusion.

Kate ran her finger over the gash from which Audrey would emerge, trying to remember what she'd been thinking, what she'd intended: Audrey emerging from her head, fully grown, wearing running shoes, wielding a spear. A wise warrior goddess, breaking away into adulthood—wasn't that it? From her plastic bag filled with wedged clay she scraped out a piece the size of a grapefruit. She rolled the damp earth between her palms, thinking about the form it would ultimately take. Then she set it on the table and kneaded it, punching down any air bubbles, pressing it with her palms, rolling it this way, then that. The process that had always excited her—the beginning of something new—now left her empty and drained.

She formed the clay into a limbless body, then pinched out the head. She did this by rote, as if hand-building a teacup for the hundredth time. When she'd curved the neck—too thin—with her thumbs, she set the misshapen form on the table. The Birth of Athena. It seemed trivial. Meaningless. Why create this piece? Why create anything at all?

She rolled the hunk of clay into a ball, set it on the table, and left. She wanted to go home. Where Luke was.

Therapy

"You're clinically depressed."

The psychiatrist is younger than Luke expected, and more informally dressed, with corduroy pants and a polo shirt (no jacket, no tie), but he has the warm dark eyes and thick brown beard of the stereotypical Freudian shrink, and Luke has been speculating whether he grew the beard to make up for his youth, his casual clothing, and his degrees not from Harvard or Stanford or UCLA but from San Diego State and Gilverton U. Dr. Vernor began asking him a barrage of questions before Luke even had the chance to tell him he had a mother, and the Q&A—which almost immediately tingled with the eeriness of a right-on psychic reading—has lasted nearly twenty minutes.

Now Luke looks at him and says, "I am?"

"Absolutely. The *Diagnostic and Statistical Manual* lists nine basic symptoms of depression. If you have five of them, you're depressed. If you have four, you're probably depressed. Luke, you have all nine."

Luke takes off his glasses and wipes them on his shirt: clean glasses might help him figure out what this means. He has all nine symptoms—he should feel like a psychopath—but instead, he feels relieved. Finally, he has something, something official, something with a name: *clinical depression*. Thank God.

"I'm clinically depressed," Luke repeats, to see how it sounds.

"Clinical depression is a disease," Dr. Vernor says slowly, as though explaining something to a dense child. "It's biochemical, and the most effective method of treatment is through psychotropic drugs. In other words, the good news is, there's medication we can give you to help. Not a cure, but something that can control the disease and alleviate the symptoms, much like insulin with diabetes."

Medication. Could it be that simple? One magic pill, and hocus pocus, the shadow is banished, the pain has disappeared, life is one big barrel of monkeys? Luke is skeptical, and also nervous. He's taken over-the-counter sleeping pills before, but this, this is his brain the doctor is talking about, and the idea of tampering with it—no matter how much trouble it's been giving him lately—is scary. "What about therapy?"

"Let me put it this way. If you come into the emergency room with terrible pain in your chest and a numbness in your left arm, and you're a male over fifty years old, we're going to give you an EKG, not talk to you about the importance of exercise and healthy eating habits. From everything you've told me, about the nature of your condition, the duration, your family history, I have no reason to believe it isn't biochemical. We'll do tests, of course, but my guess is—my very strong guess is—that the antidepressant I'm going to prescribe will help a lot."

"I don't know," Luke says. "An antidepressant. It sounds so . . ." Terrifying, he wants to say, but he settles for "extreme."

Dr. Vernor smiles in a way that makes Luke think he's heard this reservation. "I'll tell you what. Why don't we try it for three weeks and see how it goes?"

"Just three weeks?"

Dr. Vernor scribbles something on a notepad, talks about possible side effects—cotton mouth, impotence—and hands Luke an unreadable prescription that may or may not be for arsenic. He hands it to him delicately, his fingers lingering on the white paper, as though he were giving him a Breguet watch or a one-way ticket to paradise, something precious and valuable, a gift. Then, for the first time, he looks at him with sympathy and concern. "I don't mean to get your hopes up too high, Luke. But I can tell you that this has been very successful with a whole lot of patients, and it just might change your life."

Three months later, Luke is holding Audrey's hand as they walk from the pottery co-op to the park. He finds the action perfectly natural. The way their hands settle in together—creating little variations in pressure, fingers adjusting first on top, then below—makes Luke feel that they're communicating, engaging in entire silent conversations: Watch yourself now, there's a car, his hand says, squeezing tightly; and Audrey's thumb taps impatiently in reply: It's a mile away, but all right.

It's Luke's day off, and as on many of his days off since Audrey last laid eyes on her father, he spent the morning shopping for and preparing a picnic lunch. The first miracle drug didn't work—it seemed to, for a few days, until he experienced nausea and a panicky anxiety—but this new one he's been on for two months appears to be helping. He's able to function, anyway. They head toward their usual spot, beside the sagebrush and in front of the swings, and Luke spreads the blanket and arranges the food.

"Hummus?" Audrey asks.

He hands her a pita sandwich—hummus, sprouts, and sunflower seeds, her favorite—and says, "Of course."

She eats greedily for a few minutes and then, her hunger satisfied, lies back on the blanket. "Uncluke?"

Luke swallows his bite of jícama salad, preparing himself. She's going to ask him an impossible question. Do dogs fall in love? How do I know when I'm dreaming? Why do roses smell different from Brussels sprouts? What's the sound the stars make? Do cats go to heaven? Why am I me and not you?

"Yes?"

"How come you're sad?"

Luke is used to being surprised by her, but this one really startles him.

"What?"

"How come?"

"Why do you think that I'm sad?"

Audrey sits up, claps the palms of her hands to her knees. "You know what you should do? You should look at an anthill. I love to watch the ants, but I'm glad I'm not one of them. Maybe if you look at an anthill you not be so sad."

Luke gazes at her messy hair, her freckled nose, her light brown eyes. He wonders if she'll outgrow her wisdom the way she will her tennis shoes, or her love for butterflies, zebras, and swings.

"Wouldn't be," he says quietly. "You *wouldn't* be so sad. But why do you think I'm sad?"

Audrey stands. "Can I go on the swings?"

"Go ahead, go."

"See that cloud?" she asks, pointing. "I'm gonna swing right into it. Watch me, Uncluke, watch me!"

She runs to the swings, sits on a canvas seat, and pumps herself higher and higher, thrusting her face into the wind on the way up, letting her long hair trail behind her on the way down, bending then straightening her legs. He watches, absorbed. Yes, she really might swing herself into the clouds.

The first thing Dr. Vernor says when Luke comes into the office is, "Are you feeling more like yourself?"

Three weeks has turned into two years, and they're still fine-tuning his meds, still looking for the miracle combination, the holy grail, the antidepressant to end all antidepressants. A few weeks ago, Luke had something of a relapse—a general feeling of weightiness, as though gravity were doubling in his limbs—and the doctor took him off the imipramine and put him on trazodone, which seems to be lifting that gray, foggy feeling from his body and also (would he be sitting here if they weren't connected?) his mind.

"Yes," he tells Dr. Vernor, "I am." And he is. He does feel more like himself, which is to say, he feels nothing like himself, nothing like the Luke he was, anyway. (And what, exactly, did that feel like? Terrible, is all he can recall.) He feels the way he imagines normal people—people without low levels of neo-something in their blood, without grandfathers who drank themselves to death, without loose synapses straggling around like cut wires in their brain—must feel most of the time: fine. Not great, not ebullient, not high on life, just: fine. It was odd to him at first, but now he's used to it, the way he's used to Dr. Vernor's casual polo shirts and the tasteful antique painting of a ship above his mahogany desk.

"Good, good." Dr. Vernor hands Luke his questionnaire, and Luke takes a ballpoint pen out of his pocket and begins to write, as he does every week.

At what time of day do you feel best: morning, afternoon, or
    evening? Afternoon
Approximately how long does it take you to fall asleep?
    One to two hours
After how many hours do you awaken? Six to seven
Have you been experiencing any nausea? No
Trembling in the hands? No
Obsessive thinking patterns? No

And if anything keeps him on his meds, it's that one, because Luke believes his so-called shadow was nothing more than an obsessive thinking pattern, a hallucination, a result of biochemical bad wiring, and now, thanks to his drugs, the shadow has been banished, like King Lear out into the storm. There's some slippage, of course—too many milligrams of antianxiety tranquilizers, or too few—and he can feel it there, creeping up on him, lurking. But in general, the shadow has gotten smaller. It's as small as a stone, as small as a pebble, so small that sometimes Luke can almost—almost—believe it isn't there.

"**Let's** play Say Uncle," Audrey says.

They're in his apartment, doing the dishes. Audrey is washing; Luke's drying and putting away. They've been performing this chore, which should have taken but a few minutes (there are only the dinner dishes, a wok, silverware, and some glasses and mugs), for at least a quarter of an hour, because Luke put Louis Armstrong on the CD player, and every so often Audrey stops what she's doing to sing along into a pretend microphone, or do a little dance (she tries to make Luke dance with her, but he refuses), and Luke stands by, patiently waiting until she's ready to resume.

"What?" he asks.

"You know. You grab hold of someone's arm"—Audrey sets down her sponge and holds his forearm between her soapy hands—"then you twist it like you're wringing out a towel."

"Ouch."

Audrey giggles. "Then you have to say 'Uncle' for me to stop."

Luke has never thought of this as a game, but he's certainly done it before with his sisters. Colleen always said "Uncle" right away, not understanding the point of suffering for some misplaced sense of pride, while Kate would wait until tears welled in her eyes before she'd utter the magic word. Luke doesn't remember ever feeling any pain. He simply allowed his sisters to twist his skin, and then, after a suitable amount of time, yelled, "Uncle!"

Audrey twists his arm. Either she's very strong for a six-year-old or he's a twenty-nine-year-old wimp, because it certainly does sting. "Uncle!"

Audrey smiles. "Now you do it to me."

Luke twists her arm. "Harder," she tells him.

"I don't want to hurt you."

"That's the whole point. If you don't hurt me, how am I gonna say 'Uncle'?"

Luke twists harder. Her skin is turning red. "Say 'Uncle,' " he tells her.

"No!"

He imagines one of his neighbors going up or down the back steps, peering through his kitchen window, calling the cops for child abuse. "Are you sure?"

"Keep going."

He twists her arm slightly harder, feeling the fragile bone beneath his hand.

"Uncle Luke!" Audrey shouts.

Luke yanks his hands away. "Are you all right?"

Audrey laughs. "That's the game," she says, rubbing her reddened skin. "But instead of just saying 'Uncle,' I say 'Uncle Luke.' Get it?"

He isn't sure that he does. But Audrey loves the game and for months afterward begs Luke to play with her. He always refuses. He doesn't want to hurt her, he explains, and the one time he lets Audrey twist his arm, she quickly grows bored. He gives up too easily, she tells him. It isn't any fun.

One Friday afternoon, when Audrey is helping pile the leaves Luke has just raked from his mother's lawn into plastic bags, they reach what he will later think of as a turning point. Before that autumnal February day (it's chilly, they're both wearing sweaters, dry leaves are blowing all around), Audrey has never asked about Sam Monroe, and then, apropos of nothing, she says:

"What's my father like?"

Luke continues to rake, trying not to show his surprise. He thinks of his trip to Phoenix a few months after Colleen gave birth to a baby girl. He remembers the way Sam held her in his arms, cooing down at her like a daddy bird, shading her face from the sun. "He's a very fine mechanic," he says.

"A what?"

"He fixes cars very well."

"Oh. What else?"

"I guess you might say he's impetuous. He married your mother quickly, and then he did the same with your aunt. He's handsome, I believe, in a ruggedly boyish way, as they say. You have his eyes, you know."

"I do?"

"Yes. And he has quite an endearing voice. The faintest drawl. Charming. I wouldn't be at all surprised if my sisters fell in love with him because of that voice. On the other hand, he could never sing 'Happy Birthday' on key."

"Is he smart?"

"A mechanical genius."

"Nice?"

"Very. I mean, he didn't always do things that were particularly nice, but in conversation, very."

"What's his favorite color?"

"I haven't the faintest idea."

Audrey picks apart a brittle leaf from its veinous stem. "And my aunt Colleen? What's she like?"

Luke thinks for a moment. Finally he says, "Your aunt Colleen is like this rare food you didn't know you were hungry for until you tasted it, and then you can't seem to be satisfied by anything else."

"That's why my daddy married her?"

"I think so. Yes."

Audrey nods, apparently satisfied. And then suddenly, her lips pucker into a pout. "But my mommy isn't like that?"

Luke smiles. "Your mother is a goddess," he assures her. "And so are you."

Luke doesn't know if his being around someone so alive—a child, after all, filled with the joyful curiosity of discovering the world—is for him a blessing or a curse. There are times when her vivacity drains him, when watching her run in and out of the ocean, squealing for him to come join her, or listening to her talk nonstop over hot cocoa in a café, makes his own body numb, so that merely walking to the car afterward takes every ounce of energy he has. But there are other days, other moments, when her youthful exuberance is an anchor holding him to this world. Times when he thinks about the rest of his life—in the bookstore, at home reading—a life of qualified unhappiness, and feels that Audrey is a bright spot, a balm, as therapeutic, in her own way, as his medication, a glimmer of comfort and hope.

While Sam splashes with Jennifer in the shallow end of the pool, and baby Ryan takes a nap in the car seat beside Colleen's chair, Luke and Colleen talk in the shaded patio of her backyard. This is Luke's third trip to Phoenix, but the intense dry heat still shocks him, squeezes on his lungs like mountain air.

"Sam misses her," Colleen says.

Luke nods. "I bet."

"Sometimes he'll get this far-off look in his eyes, and I know he's thinking of her. Or he'll wonder out loud what she's doing, how she is. I mean, Mom sends us pictures and everything, but it's not the same."

"Maybe I should talk to Kate."

Colleen looks at him, interested. "Really?"

Luke has been thinking about this for the past few years, ever since Audrey first mentioned Sam Monroe: telling Kate that

Audrey asks about her father every so often, that he believes it would be healthy for her to get to know him. The fact that Luke even cares about this, that he now has an opinion one way or the other, that he's able to feel an emotional response, has been profoundly meaningful to him, and makes him think that perhaps he's getting better. He hasn't spoken to Kate yet because the opportunity hasn't come up, but now he tells himself that when he returns to San Pablo, he'll make it come up.

"It's been so long," he says. "If Sam wants to see his daughter, and Audrey wants to see her father—"

"Audrey wants to see Sam?"

"She's curious about him, let me put it that way."

Colleen stares off into the distant mountain shaped like a camel's back. "Growing up, I didn't miss our father, really, but I missed the idea of him, you know? I didn't miss Grady Flannigan, whoever that was. I missed having a dad." She turns to Luke. "Sam's a good father, he really is. Do you think Kate will agree?"

"She's stubborn . . ."

"As a fucking mule."

"But she has Audrey's best interests at heart, and I can say with relative certainty that seeing her father every so often would be in Audrey's best interest."

Colleen strokes Luke's cheek with the back of her fingers, the intimate gesture of a mother, or a lover. "It would make Sam so happy," she says.

Earlier that morning, Colleen mentioned that she was having an affair with a tennis pro named Troy, and Luke tries to reconcile the glowing manner in which she described for him Troy's serve with the image before him now, a devoted wife wanting nothing more than to make her husband happy. Finally he gives up. Both are equally real, equally true.

"I'll do my best," Luke assures her. "What's the worst thing she could say? No?"

"No," Kate says. "No."

They're sitting in her apartment, on the couch in front of the coffee table, which displays Kate's latest sculpture, one of Luke's favorites. It's a sphere, glazed a dark, earth-toned red, entitled *What Fall?* On top of the sphere is Eve—naked, pale, with wide hips and sagging breasts (no bras in the Garden of Eden)—standing in front of a tree, reaching up for a shiny red apple. Kate has captured on Eve's face a purity, an innocence, with just a seed of something else—not defiance, curiosity, or envy, the emotions usually ascribed to her temptation, but something more like wisdom, as though, deep down, Eve knew exactly what she was doing, and understood its necessity. Humans need knowledge, her face seems to say. We can't live in this boring garden forever.

"I'm not just relaying a message," Luke says quietly, because Audrey is sleeping in the next room. "I'm telling you what I think. I think it would be healthy for Audrey to see her father."

Kate's smile is composed, serene. "I don't care what you—pardon me—what anyone else thinks."

He sits back, wipes his forehead with his sleeve. "But Kate. Audrey is—"

"Mine. Audrey is mine." After a moment, she adds, "I'll tell you what I'll do. You carry a child in your womb for nine months, you spend eight hours in labor with her without painkillers, you sacrifice yourself for her, you catch her colds, dream her dreams, feel her pain, and then you know what I'll do? I'll mind my own business. How's that?"

This is the closest they've come to a fight since they've been adults, and he remembers how headstrong she can be; he remembers the time he didn't allow her to touch his model planes, how she didn't speak to him for three days.

"All right," he says, backing down. "I'm sure you know what's best."

Kate sighs. "I'm not sure I know what's best. But I know what's possible."

Luke gazes at his sister's profile, at the strong Gaelic nose, the prominent cheekbones, the wide lips that, on close inspection, seem to be just barely trembling. Underneath her aggressive independence, her confident self-sufficiency, Luke detects a thin strand of vulnerability and fear. She's afraid, he imagines, of the same thing he's afraid of; it's a fear so great it doesn't have a name, so complicated and amorphous it's impossible to translate into words, but if one had to, if one were forced to, one might call it fear of failure: Failing as an artist, as a mother to Audrey, as a human being. Perhaps this is something they share, as brother and sister, the way they share long fingers, flat feet, a proclivity to solitude, and an allergy to pollen.

"I'm sorry," he tells her. "You're right, it's none of my business."

She continues to gaze straight ahead, her eyes focused on a point on the pale yellow walls, or perhaps on nothing at all. Then she turns and smiles at him, gracious and forgiving. "It's okay," she says. "But do me a favor, will you?"

"Of course."

"Don't ever bring it up again."

Luke wouldn't think of it. He knows better than most people how to mind his own business. He keeps his mouth shut as Audrey goes from grade to grade—from jacks to soccer, from Roald Dahl to Isabel Allende, from Monopoly to Myst, from trips to the park with Luke to fun-and-educational outings (a jazz concert, an aquarium) with Kate's boyfriend, Alek Perez—still confused about her father.

Before Luke knows it, four more years pass. Eight long years since he started his medication. Dull, uneventful years, unless one considers the unpredictable side effects of antidepressant after antidepressant to be exciting.

The Zoloft, his latest, levels off, so Dr. Vernor switches him to Prozac, which makes his hands shake so badly he can't shelve a book, use the cash register, or go to his mom's for Friday dinner. He tells her he has a cold—just a little thing, but he doesn't want to infect anybody—since he can't explain to her that he doesn't have Parkinson's, he isn't going through heroin withdrawal, not to worry, Mom, it's just Prozac. Dr. Vernor lowers the dosage, prescribes another pill to combat the side effects, but nothing works, and so he puts him on something new, some MAO inhibitor.

He's been on this new antidepressant for about ten days when he awakens one November morning to the sound of Mrs. Weiss's coughing on the other side of his bedroom wall. It makes him nervous, almost afraid, and he wonders if it's the new drug. He's sick of these drugs. Whenever he begins to feel good, hopeful that this time, this combination, this dosage, will do the trick, his hopefulness turns into disillusion because of a relapse, a terrible new side effect—anxiety and fear over some sweet old lady's coughing—a crash. And yet he's afraid to go off the medications, afraid of what might be waiting for him if he does. His fear makes him feel dependent on them, and that makes him hate them even more.

He reaches for his glasses, and thinks, Great: it's the day of Audrey's father-daughter breakfast at school. He promised to take her and her friend Sandira, got Peter to fill in for him at the store, and now he has to go, no matter how strange he feels, because Alek is teaching at the high school, and it's too late for Kate to find some other ersatz dad.

He gets out of bed (Mrs. Weiss's coughing comes to an abrupt stop, which frightens Luke even more than the hacking did, until he hears a sudden TV laugh track), feels that he might have to go to the bathroom, can't, and then opens the medicine chest where he keeps his current vials of pills. (The others he stores in a shoe box behind the towels in the linen closet, just in case.) He washes two pills down with a sip of water, and goes to get dressed.

Audrey and Sandira squish together in the passenger's bucket seat of Luke's Toyota, and as he pulls out of Kate's new condominium complex, he thinks they must feel as awkward about going to this breakfast with him as he does. "It doesn't bother you," he asks, "to attend a father-daughter event with me?"

Audrey and Sandira exchange puzzled glances.

"Half the people in our class are going with their moms," Audrey says. "At least we're going with the right gender."

"This is end-of-the-millennium southern California," Sandira adds. "Fathers are becoming obsolete."

"Like dinosaurs," Audrey agrees.

"Or typewriters."

"Nobody has a father anymore, Uncle Luke."

Luke imagines some catastrophe that's killed all the fathers off; he imagines a matriarchal society, like that of Amazons, or elephants. "Nobody?"

"Well, some people do," Sandira says. "Greta Briar?"

"Isn't that her stepdad?"

"I heard her parents split up but then they got back together."

"That new girl Heather has a dad."

"She is such a Barbie. What about Joyce Kellerman?"

"Her dad tries to be so sweet but he's such a geek," Audrey says. "Joyce always makes these really dumb mistakes in soccer, but her dad's like, 'Nice try, Joyce!' One time he took the whole team out for ice cream."

"There's one thing about him, though," Sandira says. "He's the only dad who remembers everyone's name."

"That's true," Audrey says. "Everyone else's are total workaholics."

"You see them driving away in their Porsches and Beemers and it's like, 'Okay, Daddy-o, later!' "

Luke rolls down his window a crack. He's finding it harder and harder to breathe.

"It's cooler to go to this thing with your uncle," Audrey says, "than it is to go with your mom, or your stepdad, or your mother's boyfriend, or even your dad, if he's a jerk."

"Uncles are the coolest," Sandira agrees. "Uncles and grandpas."

"Who has a grandpa?" Audrey asks.

Sandira thinks for a moment. "I don't know."

In the cafeteria of Audrey and Sandira's school, which goes from kindergarten through eighth grade, Luke caterpillars his six-foot-two-inch frame to sit on the miniature plastic bench connected to the miniature plastic table. Now he knows how Gulliver felt. Audrey and Sandira laugh at him as he struggles to lean over his jutting knees to eat: pancakes, bacon, muffins, and scrambled eggs, served family style, so that everything's cold by the time he digs in.

He drinks two cups of coffee and a glass of orange juice, while his neighbor, Dave Rodriguez (the proud, real, honest-to-

God biological and emotional nondivorced father, Luke has learned, of a girl named Brittany), discusses the housing market with someone's mother and someone else's older brother, and Luke tries hard not to scream. His bladder is full, but he isn't sure he can stand up to go to the bathroom. His heart is palpitating, and he feels nauseated and weak. Maybe he'll have a heart attack right here, right now. His mother would blame it on the fatty institutionalized food, and Luke would be forever off the hook.

Five minutes pass. He's still alive. A teacher thanks everyone for coming and introduces the speaker—a Dr. Somebody, who's going to discuss the importance of positive male role models for girls' self-esteem—and Luke excuses himself (this isn't easy: Audrey and Dave Rodriguez have to scoot way over so he can unwind his legs, circle around, and finally stand) and walks down the hall until he finds a door marked "Boys."

He stands in front of a urinal that reaches to his knees. Nothing happens. He imagines waves crashing on the beach, the rhythmic sound of rain, water running from a faucet. His palpitations increase to all-out pounding: if he doesn't pee, right now, he's going to explode, and why in the world can't he pee? A man comes in and stands at the urinal farthest away, lets out a good long piss that makes Luke teary-eyed with envy, glances at Luke—who's just standing there, holding his dick in his hands—and then zips up his pants and gets the hell out of there, fast. Why is this happening? And can you die from not being able to take a leak?

After an eternity, Luke hears applause. Audrey and Sandira are going to wonder where he is. He walks back to the cafeteria, hunched over, sweating with anxiety.

"Are you okay?" Audrey says. Everyone is standing, milling around, leaving, or about to. "How come you were gone for so long? Where'd you go?"

"I'm fine. Couldn't find the washroom is all."

"You look kind of pale," says Sandira.

"I might be coming down with something. Maybe we should leave."

The drive to Kate's condo might be less than a mile, but it's the longest car ride he's ever taken. He drops the girls off in the driveway, tells them he has to get home, and then stops at the first pay phone he sees and calls Dr. Vernor, telling the secretary it's an emergency.

"It might be the new MAO inhibitors," Dr. Vernor says. "Urinary hesitancy is a possible side effect, but I've never heard of anyone experiencing anything like this." He sounds almost impressed.

"Yes, well. What do I do?"

Dr. Vernor gives him the name of a urologist. Luke goes inside a gas station to get more change, walking bowlegged, like a cowboy, or a honeymoon groom. He goes back to the phone, punches in the number, and explains the problem to the nurse, who tells him he should come right over. Luke can barely drive to the office building, four blocks away. As soon as he gets there, he's rushed into an examination room, where the urologist inserts a catheter into his penis. This hurts so much Luke thinks he might pass out, or else grab the stethoscope from the nurse's neck and use it to strangle himself. But the relief he immediately feels is immense, and when the catheter's removed, his dick still throbbing with pain and his heart still pounding in his chest, he swears to himself that he's never going to take another goddamn pill as long as he lives.

This might be nothing more than impulsive bravado, but it's not. That evening, as he boils some water to make pasta, he feels anxious and weak, and he has to turn off the stove and lie down on the couch. He places his hand on his heart, which is pounding too fast, and then too slow. He holds his breath, feeling his heartbeat become slower and slower, and then—he can't last any longer—breathes out. He tries to imagine being dead. That amniotic expanse of pure nothingness, like the time before he was born. How pleasant. He takes off his glasses, rubs the pinched indentations on his nose, and is amazed by what a thin layer of skin there is between the bone and his fingers. How long would it take for that skin to rot away?

He makes a mental note to write "yes" after *Obsessive thinking patterns?* on next week's questionnaire, and then remembers he isn't going to fill out any more questionnaires, because he isn't going back to Dr. Vernor. He's tired, not just of the side effects—he could live with those, if the antidepressants really helped—but of feeling like nothing more than a sea sponge with electrical and chemical impulses controlled by licit drugs. He's tired of not knowing who is Luke and who is the pharmaceutical cocktail blended by his bartender, Dr. Vernor. He's tired of feeling there is no difference between the two.

He leaves a message on Dr. Vernor's machine saying that he isn't coming in on Wednesday, that he isn't coming to see him anymore, and he's relieved that he's managed to do this without actually speaking to him. But when the phone rings an hour later, it's his shrink.

"Luke? I got your message. Listen, I know you had a really bad experience today, and I'm sorry about that. But we can try—"

"It's not that," Luke says. "It's not only what happened today. It's everything. I just don't think it's working anymore." He pauses, then says, "I'm going off the meds."

Dr. Vernor's voice is gentle and concerned: "Luke. You're clinically depressed. You can't do that."

Luke shuts his eyes. Dr. Vernor has listened to every fluctuation in his moods, every wavering symptom, every microscopic change in his body and mind, for an hour a week for more than eight years, and even though Luke's insurance company has paid him well for the privilege, he's the closest thing Luke has to a nonrelated friend.

"I appreciate all your help, Dr. Vernor," he says. "All your concern. But I'm not asking your permission. I'm telling you, I have to do this on my own. Good-bye."

He hangs up before the doctor can respond, and goes into the bathroom, grabs the almost full vial of new MAO inhibitors from the medicine chest, and flushes them down the toilet. Then he takes down the shoe box, and one by one unpops the lids off the brown vials, and tosses all the other antidepressants into the bowl as well. Blue, green, yellow, red: a rainbow of oval and circular pills floats on the water and sinks to the porcelain bottom, dozens and dozens, maybe even a hundred pills. He flushes the toilet, and watches them swirl away. He imagines them traveling through the sewers, emptying into the ocean, decomposing until they become one with the Pacific. He feels excited, terrified, but most of all, most of all, he feels free.

Visitation

Audrey was sitting on the metal bleachers, staring at the base-ball diamond—it was October, and no one was around (though she could hear noise from the nearby football field and track)—thinking about all the people who had once made home runs, flied out, missed balls, run around the dusty bases to get tagged on second or slide into home, and about how these vivid moments had simply vanished, the field was empty, and she had no idea who those people were or what had happened to them. It was like, every second was always on the brink of becoming history (that one was gone, and now that one, now that one), and it made her feel really weird to think of all those lost moments she had no memory of, all those hours that she hadn't been with Uncle Luke—thousands and thousands of them—that only he'd known about, and now that he was dead, they were just gone.

She glanced at her watch and decided it was safe to walk home. She picked up her backpack, went out the open gates, and hurried across the street, because her team was practicing on the track and she didn't want Coach Bryant to see her. Not that it was any big deal—she wasn't ditching practice, she'd quit—but Coach might think it was strange that she was hanging around the empty baseball bleachers after school, and maybe she'd say something to Alek about it, and then Alek would say something to her mom, and then her mom would find out that she wasn't on the cross-country team anymore. Which also wouldn't be that big a deal, except that it was none of her mom's business.

It was kind of warm, and sunny, and walking home, she almost felt good—she almost forgot that her life was a total mess—but then she got to the corner of Hacienda and Fifth, which was where her aunt Colleen had unknowingly divulged her mom's big secret. It had been four days, and Audrey could still hear her aunt's words, the sound of her voice, breezy and low, inside her own head. Audrey had said, "I wish we could go visit you in Phoenix, but I know Mom will never take us."

And Aunt Colleen had replied, "Don't be too hard on your mom. We hurt her a lot, your father and I did, and I understand her . . . reaction. Not that he hasn't paid for it—your dad really misses you a lot. But don't worry." She'd taken one hand off the wheel to pat Audrey's knee, like an aunt. "One of these days your mom'll come around and let you and your father see each other again. Just wait."

Audrey had given Colleen a smile worthy of an Academy Award–winning actress, as if her aunt hadn't been telling her anything she didn't already know, as if she hadn't just found out she'd been betrayed, the naive victim inside some huge web of conspiracy, as if she hadn't just discovered that she'd been lied to by everyone she'd ever loved: her mom, most of all, but also her grandma, Alek, and even Uncle Luke.

"Hi," her mom said. She was kneeling on the edge of the front lawn—which practically came up to Audrey's ankles—weeding the flowers around the border without gloves, so that her hands were familiarly dirty, but with soil, not clay, and mud-brown. "How was school?"

"Fine."

A week before, her mom would have called her on an answer like that—she would have jokingly pestered her until Audrey elaborated, or at least gave a more revealing adjective—but now she merely nodded and returned to her weeding.

Audrey began to walk inside, but her mom called her back.

"Yeah?"

"Do you . . . do you think I should water the lawn?"

This was how her mom had become: like a pancake, like a little kid. Audrey had no idea what her mom did all day while she was at school, but in the evenings, she was always doing what looked pretty much like nothing. Staring off into space. Watching TV. Spending about an hour chopping an onion and then saying to Alek, "What was I making again?" And Alek would answer, "Split-pea soup," or, "An omelet," really gently, like she had Alzheimer's or something and he was her long-suffering spouse.

"No, Mom, I think the grass is long enough already," Audrey said, and went into the house.

She wanted to go to her room, to see Rosie, who was probably waiting for her there, on her bed, but knew that she should go say hello to her grandmother first. She tucked in her stomach and readied herself before she knocked on the study door.

"Grandma?"

Her grandmother didn't say anything, and after a few seconds, Audrey turned the knob and looked in. Her grandmother was sitting at her desk in front of the computer; newspapers were spread around her; pages were coming out of the fax machine and falling to the carpeted floor. Her mom and Alek had thought it was so great when her grandma had left her vigil by the window the day before to do some work, but it was obvious to Audrey that she'd simply traded one mysterious obsession for another. Her grandma's face was hard, her jaw set, as she viciously typed into the computer.

"Do you need anything, Grandma?" Audrey asked.

Her grandmother stopped typing only to look over a fax, and Audrey said, "Okay, then. Well, I'll see you."

She waited a few seconds, and finally her grandma turned around—she looked like she was trying to smile but had forgotten how—and then half nodded and closed the door. She went upstairs to find Rosie, the only living thing she felt comfortable around nowadays, the only mammal that made sense to her anymore.

Audrey spent most of the weekend in her room—in her uncle's old room—doing homework, listening to music, petting Rosie. For about an hour she stared at her uncle's will, trying to figure out what he'd been thinking, as if her mom would care about a bunch of plates when he was dead, or her grandma would ever be like, "Oh, I think I'll play some music on my son's CD player now." Mostly, she tried to avoid spending any time with her mom or Alek—who was there constantly—and she was pretty successful at it.

Until Sunday, when there was a knock on her door, and she heard Alek's voice. "Audrey?"

"Yeah?"

"Can I come in?"

Audrey was lying on her bed, reading *Julius Caesar* for English, wearing a pair of flannel PJ bottoms and a gray tank top—it didn't matter, Alek had seen her in pajamas a million times—and even though she didn't feel like dealing with him, what was she supposed to say?

"Sure."

He entered and walked around the room, picking things off the bookshelf and setting them down, which kind of bugged her. Then he leaned against the desk and looked at her. "I was thinking. It's been a long time since we've done anything together, just the two of us. I thought maybe you might like to go out for breakfast."

She held up her book. "I'm reading."

"We don't have to go for that long."

"Did Mom put you up to this?"

Alek smiled. "I haven't told her yet."

"I don't think so," she said. "But thanks."

"I'd like to know what's going on with you. You've become Audrey the Great Big Mystery, you know."

"Sorry to disappoint you, but there's no mystery here. I'm just trying to read. That's all."

Alek let a few seconds pass before he spoke. "Fair enough. But if you ever feel like talking to someone, and you don't want to talk with me or your mom, you can always go see Dr. Miller. And of course, we can also take you to see someone who specializes in grief counseling."

The word "we" echoed in Audrey's mind. Was he talking about himself and her mom, or him and her, and if it was him and her mom, was he trying to be some kind of parent? And then she thought of going to see Dr. Miller, the part-time shrink at the school, who specialized in eating disorders but who weighed about ninety-nine pounds herself, or some grief counselor, someone who would try to figure out what stage of grief she was in and give her this look all gooey with concern and ask, "How do you feel?"

"Thanks," she told him. "I'll keep it in mind."

Alek straightened, and gestured toward her book. "What are you reading, anyway?" he asked, trying to act normal.

"*Hamlet,*" she said, just to torture him.

He looked kind of surprised, but he nodded, and left the room.

Audrey woke up early on Monday and walked to school, so she wouldn't have to ride in the car with her mom, and there, on the front steps, she saw Blaine Durbin, writing something in a notebook, probably lyrics to a new song. For the first time she thought of what a cliché it was for her to have a crush on a guy in a band, someone who rode a motorcycle and wrote lyrics in black notebooks. He stretched his arms over his head, and Audrey caught a glimpse of pale skin between his jeans and faded Nirvana T-shirt, a line of coarse black hair below his navel, and she remembered thinking how sexy his stomach was when she'd seen it once before, but now it seemed like nothing but a stomach, pale and thin and gross. He saw her— she was only wearing baggy jeans and an old black sweatshirt, but she didn't care—and he smiled and said, "Audrey," like he'd only now remembered she existed, which he probably had.

"Help me out, will you?" he asked.

"With what?"

"I'm forging an absentee note. What should I have been sick with on Friday?"

"The flu?"

He shook his head. "I had that last week."

"What about food poisoning?"

"Good one. Very topical."

The ten-minute bell rang. Audrey said, "Hope you feel better," and walked away, but when Blaine said, "Wait," she turned around. "I'm sorry about your uncle," he told her, his pale gray eyes staring into hers.

Audrey kept looking at him—how did he know? and why did he care?—and then lowered her eyes and said, "Thanks."

There was this moment in geometry when she thought of how weird it was that all the people in this room happened to be alive at the same time, and how instead of trying to get to know one another or even just commenting on this strange fact—it was like, thousands of centuries had passed, millions even, and maybe would pass again, and there they were, in the same town, the same school, the same room—Mr. Monotone just droned on and on and Sara Paulie passed a note to this guy Brian and Warner raised his hand to every question and Amanda Hayes said, "I don't know," when Mr. Monotone called on her, because she thought that it was feminine or something to act like a total airhead, and Audrey just wanted to stand up and say, *Who are you?* But it was stupid—not because you couldn't stand up and force people to answer your dumb questions, of course you couldn't, and not even because maybe it was something you couldn't even really know about yourself, much less explain to another person, but because what difference did it make? In three hundred years, no one would know they'd ever existed. In a hundred years, they'd be nothing but fading memories in the minds of their senile children. In eight or nine decades, every last one of them would be dead.

"**Oh** my God," Sandira said, grabbing Audrey's wrist as soon as she got to their locker. "I had the most terrible dream last night. I was wrapped in gauze, you know, like a mummy? and all of these bats swooped down on me, and I kept calling, 'Uncle Luke, Uncle Luke,' and he kept yelling, 'I'm coming, hold on, I'm coming,' but he never came." Sandira paused dramatically. "I'm telling you, it was totally terrifying."

In the week and a half since Luke had died, Sandira had been having these bad nightmares just about every night, but it was kind of hard to feel sorry for her, because she'd also been watching a lot of scary movies. Whenever Audrey called her, she was all, "I've got to go, I'm in the middle of *The Shining*" or *The Omen* or *Scream*—which she said she watched because it was almost Halloween, but she never used to watch horror movies every night around Halloween, and Audrey thought it was all too weird.

"Maybe if you'd stop watching horror movies you wouldn't have bad dreams."

"Thank you, Dr. Freud. The thing is, I kind of like dreaming about your uncle. Even if it does freak me out."

"Are you done in here?"

Sandira nodded. She still had her nose stud in and everything, but she was just wearing a flannel shirt, and except for her maroon hair, she looked kind of normal.

Audrey shut the locker. "I'll see you at lunch," she said.

"Let's meet at that bench, okay?"

All last week, Sandira had been trailing her around like some sad puppy, saying stuff like, "I wonder if Uncle Luke ever ate at this table," and, "Isn't it weird to think that Uncle Luke used to walk these same halls?" and sometimes Audrey had just wanted to shake her and say, Get a grip. And then Sandira had found this bench on the patio above the outdoor cafeteria that had the initials L.F. carved into the seat, and even though Uncle Luke wasn't the sort of person to carve his initials into a bench—

he wasn't even the sort of person to own a pocketknife—Sandira had been totally awed by the coincidence and had insisted they eat there again.

"Do you know how many people probably went to this school whose initials were L.F.?"

"Please?"

"About a million," Audrey told her. But Sandira was making her eyes really big, and when the warning bell rang, Audrey finally said, "Yeah, all right, whatever," just so she wouldn't be late to class.

"**How** was your day?"

Audrey had come into the kitchen, where her mom was brewing tea. "Well, I'm not Chuck Brewster," she heard her grandma say from the next room. "I'll get that zoning, mark my words. If I have to buy this whole goddamn town, I'll get zoning. If I have to run for mayor myself, I'll—"

"Fine," Audrey said.

Her mom smiled nervously and asked, "Fine good or fine rotten?" but it sounded forced.

"Just fine," Audrey told her. She waited, refusing to blink. A line came into her mind, from a western, or a song, or maybe it was just a saying: *You can run but you can't hide.* Audrey thought these words, staring at her, until her mother looked away.

On Thursday, Audrey stayed around the bleachers until close to six—there was a meet that day, a home meet—and then she walked to her grandma's. As soon as she opened the door, she knew that something was wrong. It was quiet, too quiet, almost silent, which didn't make any sense, because Alek's minivan was in the driveway, which meant that they should have been talking, watching the news, making dinner—something. She set down her backpack and slowly walked into the kitchen, where her mom was leaning against the counter, her arms crossed, like she'd been waiting for her. Alek was sitting at the kitchen table; he gave her a helpless, fatalistic look.

"What?" Audrey said.

"Where were you today?"

"School."

"And then where?"

Audrey knew that she was busted, but she didn't care. "Why?"

"Because I'm your mother, and you're thirteen years old, and I think I have a right to know. Alek and I went to watch your meet today. Imagine my surprise when Coach Bryant told me you'd quit." She shook her head. "I'm not mad at you for quitting the team, Audrey. I'm mad because you lied to me."

"I didn't lie to you, Mom. I just didn't answer a question you didn't ask."

"Don't quibble with me, Audrey. Why didn't you tell me?"

"Why didn't I tell you? Why didn't I tell you I quit the cross-country team? Gee, Mom, I don't know, why didn't you tell me my father wanted to see me? Why didn't you tell me that you were the one who kept us apart? That maybe, just maybe, my father actually loved me? 'I quit the cross-country team,' 'Your father loves you.' Let's see, which is the more important omission? Who, exactly, is the liar in this family?"

Her mom paused, surprised. Then this expression of understanding gradually spread over her face, and she said, "So that's what this is all about."

"What?"

"The way you've been acting. I see your aunt filled you in on our family history—her side of it, anyway."

"All she did was tell me the truth. Which, by the way, she assumed I already knew."

Her mom turned to Alek, who looked at her like he was there to lend moral support but really couldn't get involved, and then she frowned and said, "It was complicated. I was always going to tell you someday. When you asked, when you'd gotten older."

"I am older, Mom."

Her mom was kind of rebuked, put in her place, but then she sighed and said, "Audrey, your father is not this hero—"

"Do you think I don't know that? Do you think I'm stupid? I don't want a hero, I just want . . ."

What she wanted was the right to judge for herself. No, what she wanted was her entire life back, because it hadn't been real: every little thing in it—playing hopscotch, reading books, having picnics with her mom or Uncle Luke—was subsumed now by her mother's lie. Everyone's lie.

"What difference does it make what I want? Obviously, it's never made any before."

Her mom didn't say anything. She seemed tired, and her hair, tied back in a low ponytail, was greasy. "You don't understand," she said.

"I understand that you're a liar."

"Audrey." Alek rose. "Listen, I know that you're upset—"

"You don't know anything! You're just my mother's boyfriend. Okay? You're nothing to me."

Audrey had wanted to hurt him—this sidekick of her mother's who must have known everything and kept everything from her, right along with her mom—but he just looked like, okay, he'd seen arguments like this a thousand times and wasn't about to get worked up over this one, like he was willing to forgive and forget. Water off a duck's back, he always said—which kind of pissed her off, because why weren't they taking her seriously? Why didn't they see that she was serious, dead serious, that she wasn't just some little kid causing a scene?

"Audrey . . ." her mother began.

"Leave me alone," Audrey said, backing up. "Both of you, just leave me alone."

She stood in her closet and opened the door to the attic, then she pulled out a bag that had belonged to Uncle Luke. It was blue canvas, Lands' End, a carry-on bag, which would be perfect: light enough to carry to the bus station, and inconspicuous while she walked around wherever she was going. Phoenix, maybe. Or maybe she'd just hop on the next bus out of town.

She tossed the bag on her bed—she was trembling, from anger or excitement, or maybe both—took out her uncle's sweaters that were inside, and stuffed them into a near-empty drawer of the bureau. A brown one caught her eye—an old cardigan she'd never seen him wear, with a few moth holes and a missing button—and she put it on. It came down to her thighs, its sleeves to her fingernails. It was soft, warm, tough.

She threw some underwear, socks, T-shirts, and pants into the bag, but then she sat on the edge of the bed, dropped the bag to the floor, and buried her face in her hands (which smelled metallic—the bleachers). She felt like all the air had been sapped out of her, a pin poking into a balloon. What was she supposed to do? Just show up at her father's garage? Hi, um, you don't know me, but my name is Audrey, I'm, uh, your daughter? Yeah, right.

She heard footsteps, a pause, knocking, her mom's voice: "Audrey?"

She pushed the bag under her bed with her foot. "What?"

Her mother opened the door. She looked calm and serene and self-righteous, and also beautiful—she always looked more beautiful after a fight, more tender, more raw—and Audrey had this image of her and Alek around a Christmas tree, married, fondling their baby, but her mom seemed a little sad, as though wondering where Audrey was.

"I'm sorry I hurt you," she said. "I didn't mean to, really. I was so hurt myself. I don't think there's any way you can understand. My husband and my sister . . ." But the way she said it, with astonishment in her voice, it sounded to Audrey that she was trying to remember herself why it had been so painful. "Your uncle Luke thought that I should allow your father to see you. So did your grandma. I thought you should know that, so you wouldn't . . . so you wouldn't blame anybody else."

"Okay," Audrey said. "I won't."

"I only did it out of love for you."

"Because you loved me, or because you hated my dad?"

Her mom actually seemed to be thinking about this. "I don't know anymore. The two were so intertwined. Hate isn't the opposite of love, you know. Indifference is. Hatred is a passion all its own."

Audrey didn't want to hear any stupid words of wisdom from her mother, even any real, honest-to-goodness Truths, capital T, because whatever they were, they were way too late.

"I suppose you still hate him," Audrey said, not that she cared.

An expression came over her mom's face, like she didn't know whether to laugh or cry. "Audrey, my brother killed himself. How could I possibly hate your father now?"

Even when Halloween didn't mean anything to you—even when you were too old to trick-or-treat and too young to go to some wild party—you still woke up knowing this was the day. Halloween. All Hallows' Eve. Just before All Souls' Day. She'd gone to church with her grandma on that holy day once. You had to leave the church and then come back in and say a certain number of Our Fathers and Hail Marys and Audrey forgot what else, and then whoever you were praying for was put to rest. Her grandma had been praying for Grandpa Grady, which hadn't made any sense, because he'd been dead for years, and she must have done this before, but when Audrey had asked about it, her grandmother told her that when it came to the souls of men you couldn't be too careful. Audrey wondered if her grandma would go to church to pray for her husband and son, and thought, Probably not. She hadn't been to church since Uncle Luke died.

Jack-o'-lanterns decorated people's porches, and some houses were draped with fake spider webs, or cheesy store-bought decorations in the windows, and at school a few people were wearing costumes and the goths were totally decked out. The girls were wearing their fanciest ripped lace dresses, and the guys were wearing white makeup and blood-red lipstick, and one of them had on this long black cape that flowed behind him like a wedding train.

Blaine Durbin was standing by the drinking fountain after English, like he was waiting for her or something, because after he said, "Audrey, hey," and she said, "Hi," and kept walking, he actually followed her and tugged on her sleeve until she stopped.

"What's the hurry?" he said.

"I have to go to my locker."

"Wait." She looked down at his hand, which was still holding on to the baggy sleeve of her sweater—she was wearing Uncle Luke's cardigan over a black tank top—and finally he let go. "My band's playing at a Halloween party tonight. At Kenna Mathison's. I was wondering if you were going."

His eyes were the color of the sky in the morning when it was foggy out. She thought about how much this would have meant to her two weeks before—she would have rushed over to Sandira and said, "Oh my God, guess what!"—but now, she was just like, So? and she thought it was totally banal of him to like her just because she wasn't all that interested in him anymore, or maybe because her uncle had killed himself, which lent some aura of dark intrigue to her or something, which would be more than banal, it would be kind of sick.

"Kenna Mathison," Audrey said. "I don't really know her."

"It's not that kind of party. Besides, you know me."

He smiled at her, and she smiled back, but her heart wasn't in it, she was just playing the game. "All right, well, maybe I'll see you there."

"All right," Blaine said, still smiling.

Audrey walked to the locker. Sandira was standing in front of it. She was wearing a black fitted tee, black jeans, and this sparkly purplish-black lipstick, and when she saw Audrey, her face became really sad, and Audrey couldn't take it anymore, and she said, "God, Sandira, get over it, will you?"

Sandira shook her head. "I don't understand you anymore. I mean, your uncle killed himself, and you act totally unfazed, like it doesn't even affect you."

"Just because I don't dress like I'm in mourning, or moon over some stupid initials in some stupid bench—"

"It's not just that, it's everything. It's like, you don't want to talk about him. You don't want to talk about anything."

Audrey thought of what her uncle had told her once—all language is a translation—and she wished that people could just flay open their souls. But then again, maybe she didn't want anyone peering inside her soul.

"It's like you said," Audrey told her. "I'm totally unaffected."

"Wait," Sandira said. "I didn't mean it that way."

But Audrey was already walking down the hall.

It was strange, but after school, instead of taking the side streets to her grandma's, she went down Harbor Boulevard, just to try something new, she supposed, or maybe to draw out the time until she got home. She passed a lot of ethnic food shops and a gas station and a restaurant with a guy standing outside wearing a sheet over his head with two eyes cut out—"Boo!" he yelled at her, and she yelled back, "Boo, yourself"—and then her bank. She'd gone a half-block when she thought that maybe she should go in and close her account, just in case. It wasn't her big account—not the trillions of dollars her grandma had tied up in CDs and investments for her to go to college—it was only her personal savings account, but she had saved about every penny anyone had given her since she was born, and she had a little over three thousand dollars in there.

She closed the account, exchanged all but three hundred dollars for traveler's checks, and walked the rest of the way home feeling happy and light, as if she had a sweet secret she didn't want to share. Which she did.

The first trick-or-treater came to the house at around six, a kid in a grown-up's leather jacket and a plastic Elvis mask, along with his dad, who was wearing a cap that read "This is my costume." Audrey was sitting on a lawn chair on the porch—ever since she and Sandira had stopped trick-or-treating it had been her job to pass out candy at her grandmother's—and she held out the bowl, filled with Snickers and little bags of M&M's.

The kid scooped up a handful, but his dad said, "Just take one," and the boy dropped everything except a Snickers. "Now say thank you," the dad said, and the boy said, "Thank you!" really loud, like he thought maybe no one could hear him under his mask.

"You're welcome, Elvis," Audrey said.

A bloody cheerleader came up the walkway with Joan of Arc. They were followed by a gang of boys—a werewolf, the Cigarette-Smoking Man, and a can of Bud—who yelled, "Trick or treat, smell my feet, give me something good to eat!" and Audrey remembered the last time she and Sandira had gone trick-or-treating. They'd planned to go with their friend Lisa as the three Weird Sisters from *Macbeth,* but at the last minute Lisa had gotten sick, and so she and Sandira had gone as witches, with black capes and pointy hats and warts all over their noses, and brooms that kept getting in the way. That was two years ago, and they'd been kind of wild, running from house to house in their lace-up witch's boots, yelling "Trick or treat!" at the top of their lungs, leaving dirt balls on porches where you could tell people were home but didn't want to answer their doorbells. At the end of the night, they'd spilled their pillowcases filled with candy on her grandma's floor, and had eaten Milky Ways and Raisinets—their favorites—until their teeth had buzzed with sugar.

"Happy Halloween," Alek said, arriving on the porch, smiling, as though he'd forgotten all about the day before. "How's it going?"

"Okay."

A bunny rabbit came up the walkway holding hands with King Kong. "Trick or treat."

"Don't fool around," Alek told Audrey. "Hand over the candy to King Kong and maybe the bunny won't get hurt."

The kids laughed. Alek stole a bag of M&M's and said, "Let me know if you need replenishments," then went inside.

A jailbird and a cop, handcuffed together, presented themselves, followed by a girl in a sexy Middle Eastern outfit with what could have been her big brother, who was, he explained, the Victim of a Senseless Crime. He had ketchup all over his shirt and a gory plastic mask with a pierced-out eye. A carload of older guys drove by, yelling and throwing water balloons. When things had quieted down, at about eight-thirty, Audrey went inside. Her grandmother was in her study—the light was on, and Audrey could hear the clicking of a keyboard—and Alek and her mom were in the living room, sharing a big bowl of popcorn in front of an Hercule Poirot mystery on TV. Rosie was curled up in her mom's lap, and Audrey thought, Traitor. Then, for some reason, seeing her there so contented, she felt kind of glad. Kind of relieved.

"Wanna join us?" her mom asked.

"How 'bout some popcorn?" Alek said.

"No, thanks," Audrey replied, to both questions. She understood this was how it was going to be from now on. They were all going to go on like nothing had happened. Her mom would never bring up her father again, and Alek would act as if Audrey had never told him that he was nothing to her. Her grandma would stay locked up in that room, burying herself in her work so she wouldn't need to think about her son (burying herself, Audrey thought, as though she were the one who was dead), and her mom would keep putting off going back to their condo, so that she could keep sitting around watching TV. In two hours, or five months, or ten years, everything would be exactly the same. "Wanna join us?" her mom would ask. "How 'bout some popcorn?" Alek would say. "No," Audrey would still tell them. No, no, no.

She went upstairs and finished packing her bag. She couldn't stand to be in this house, with her mother, any longer. It wasn't that she hated her or was even all that angry with her anymore—she'd been angry with her for a long time, but now the anger was gone, it had floated away. It was more like her mom, and also her grandma and Alek and Sandira and everyone at school, had become strangers to her, not even acquaintances, but strangers, people she had never seen in her life, and if they were strangers, then she had nothing to say to them, and they had nothing to say to her. If they were strangers, then she might as well be around real strangers, who wouldn't pretend that they weren't.

She put her address book in the zippered compartment, because she wanted the number of this girl Zelda—a friend of Sandira's older sister—who lived in Berkeley, and had told Audrey to look her up if she was ever in town. Zelda had a fake

ID, and a frog tattooed on her ankle, and Audrey thought she was the sort of person who wasn't quite on the edge herself but knew where it was, someone who could help her get her own fake ID, maybe even help her find a place to live. As for a job, Audrey knew that she could always get one peeling potatoes or cleaning houses, the kind of exploitation jobs Mexicans were illegally hired for all the time. She went into her mom's room and stole her pink lace Wonderbra, and then packed some makeup and her own short black skirt and clunky heels, because she could probably look eighteen, a legal adult, if she tried hard enough, and she didn't want any snoopy landladies or potential employers calling the child welfare office or something. She crammed Paw-Paw, her stuffed polar bear, on top of everything, and stored the bag safely under the bed.

At a little before eleven, her mom knocked on her door. "Audrey?" she said. "Are you awake?"

"Come in." Audrey grabbed a book from her nightstand (Margaret Atwood's latest novel, which Uncle Luke had given her a few months before), because she hadn't really been doing anything—just sitting up in bed, thinking, making plans—and this might look odd to her mom.

Her mom sat in the chair next to the bed. Her hair fell in her face, and Audrey noticed strands of gray around her temples.

"Can I ask you something?" she said.

"What?"

"Why did you quit the cross-country team?"

Audrey thought back to the last time she had gone for a run, the Monday after her uncle had killed himself, the day after his funeral. Coach had made them run up to Pacific, west to Vista del Mar, the trail above the ocean, then down Harbor, and to Third, where they turned and went uphill to the school. It was one of Audrey's favorite runs, partly because of the length, three and a half miles, which was long enough for you to get into your stride but not so long that you became really tired, but mostly because she loved the mile-and-a-half stretch above the sea. The ocean breeze kicked the saltwater up to your face, and the sea-gulls cawed above your head, stretching their wings out lazily, languidly, like they were going nowhere in a hurry, and you could pace yourself by the ocean tide, feeling that you were connected to it, that the blood coursing through your veins and the air going in and out of your lungs were the tide's rhythmic cousins, like they recognized one another, and everything together made you feel strong and young and happy to be alive.

But that Monday, it hadn't been like that. Everything had seemed kind of menacing—the ocean, the seagulls, even the salt on her tongue—and Audrey hadn't been able to rise above her body, above its tiredness and pain, and she'd thought, What's the point? Not, What's the point of running when Uncle Luke is dead?—it wasn't some big existential crisis or anything like that—but more like, What's the point of running when it isn't fun? And she'd known that it was more than just a bad day, because whenever she'd had bad days before, she was itching to run again the next morning, kind of to make up for it, but this time she hadn't wanted to run the next day, or the one after that, or the one after that, and so she'd just quit.

"It's hard to explain," Audrey said. "I guess I didn't really feel like it anymore."

Her mom nodded. "I think I know what you mean. I haven't been able to get to my ceramics either. I guess I keep waiting to wake up one day with the sudden inspiration that everything once again makes sense. But sometimes . . . sometimes I'm not sure it ever will."

Her mom usually didn't talk to her like this—she didn't expose her vulnerabilities in front of Audrey—and it made her feel uncomfortable, like they were equals instead of mother and daughter. Besides, she thought her mom had it all wrong. You didn't just wake up one day and find that everything suddenly made sense again—you had to impose a sense on everything, which was hard, and tiring, and maybe, it occurred to her, this was why her uncle had killed himself. Maybe he'd gotten tired of trying to make everything make sense. Maybe it had just been too much work.

But Audrey was leaving, she might not see her mother again for a long, long time, and so she told her, "I'm sure it will, Mom. I'm sure you'll be able to get to work again soon."

Her mom sort of smiled. "You know, I didn't want you to find out about what happened the way you did, but now that it's over, I'm glad we cleared the air. I feel, well, relieved."

Audrey smiled dutifully, a girl making up with her mother, a girl about to fall asleep in her bed.

"I love you, Aud-pod," her mom said, kissing her on the cheek. "Good night."

"Good night, Mom."

It was after midnight when Audrey tiptoed down the stairs. Rosie had never come up to her room, but maybe it was just as well, because Audrey didn't know how she'd be able to say good-bye. She opened the front door quietly, shut it behind her, and then went and stood on the sidewalk. The lawn was really bad now. Dandelions had sprouted up all over the place and weeds were edging onto the concrete, and maybe because it was Halloween, or maybe because it wasn't natural—grass didn't grow this high, this fast—it looked spooky, the kind of house where little kids say a witch lives or something, just because the grass is so long and untended. Audrey wondered why her grandmother didn't want anyone to mow it—a couple of days before, her mom had brought it up again, and her grandma had been like, No, end of discussion—and she just stared at the house for a minute or so, hoping her grandma would be all right. Then she felt exposed standing on the sidewalk like that, and she hurried toward downtown.

The Trailways station was in the worst part of San Pablo, and Audrey pulled her jacket around herself and clutched her bag more tightly as she walked past people collapsed on the side of the building and a guy talking on a cellular phone who gave her the once-over. She opened the door to the station, which smelled like exhaust fumes, and went up to the man selling tickets.

"I'd like to buy a ticket to Santa Cruz," she said, because she wasn't stupid—she knew her mom would come looking for her, and if this guy remembered her he'd say she'd gone to Santa Cruz. Once she got there, she could buy another ticket to San Francisco.

"Round trip?"

"One-way."

"Your bus leaves on platform ten at six-fifteen A.M.," the man said, handing her some change and a white ticket.

"Six-fifteen," Audrey repeated, glancing at her watch—it was twelve twenty-five. "Don't you have anything earlier than that?"

"I'm afraid that's it."

Audrey thanked him and went to the large tinted window—you could see out, but not in—and sat down in one of the black seats. They were all connected, and if she lay down on three or four of them, no one would see her without walking over to this row and really looking. Besides, who would come look? It was Saturday. Her mom wouldn't even wake up before ten, and by that time, Audrey would probably already be in Santa Cruz, changing buses, maybe even on her way to San Francisco.

She set her bag on a seat, rested her head on top of it, and closed her eyes.

"Uncle Luke. What are you doing here?"

He was crouched directly in front of her, staring at her, with this weird expression on his face, almost like he was amused, and then she remembered that he was dead, and she sat up, afraid.

"I thought you were dead."

"No, no, I'm not dead." He straightened and sat in the seat next to her—he smelled of pine-scented aftershave, Irish Spring soap, and something else, something fruity and acidic, which it took her a second to realize was red wine. "I'm not dead," he added, "but I'm not exactly alive."

He was wearing khaki pants and a white dress shirt, and now she saw that he was kind of shadowy, not really real: he was there, but not there. She reached out to touch his arm, but her fingers passed right through him. "What are you?" she whispered.

He gave her a sheepish smile. "I suppose I'm something like the Invisible Man."

"But I can see you."

"Now you can, because you're dreaming. But when you wake up, I'll shout your name at the top of my lungs, and you'll ignore me. I'll shake you by the shoulders, and you won't feel a thing. I'll concentrate all my will on slamming your bedroom door, and nothing will happen. I'll . . ." His voice trailed off, and he looked sad.

"I don't feel like I'm dreaming," she told him.

"I don't fully understand the physics of it myself."

"But why aren't you . . . ? You know. Dead. Or in heaven. Or waiting to be reincarnated. Or wherever you're supposed to be."

He seemed embarrassed. He looked down at his hands,

turned them over, examining his fingernails. "Unfinished business and all that, I suppose." He paused, then said, "Listen, I was wondering if I might ask you a favor."

She imagined some mysterious potion she had to make, or maybe she had to go to her grandma's church and say those prayers, or maybe there was some message he needed her to relay, and she felt nervous and important, like he was depending on her so he could rest in peace.

"Anything," she told him.

"I was wondering if you might mow your grandmother's lawn."

"What?"

His eyes looked exactly the way they had in real life—small beneath his glasses, and sad, but in a wise, old person's way—and he shrugged and said, "I forgot. I forgot all about it. I was meaning to, but . . . and now—I know this might be hard for you to understand—I find it quite unsettling. The grass growing, and growing, and growing . . . trying to get back at me." He was staring off, as if he'd forgotten she was there, and he shivered, then turned to her and said, "Now listen. To get it going, you have to pull the cord just right—hard, but not too hard. If you pull it too hard it gets rather stubborn and refuses to budge. Hard but gentle, if you know what I mean. There's plenty of gas, so you don't need to worry about that."

"But Uncle Luke—"

"Yes?"

She gestured around the bus station. "I was planning on leaving."

He looked at her for a moment, then nodded. "Yes, well. If you can't do it, you can't do it. You have other plans. I understand."

"Maybe I can call someone for you," she told him.

He smiled vaguely. "Sure, sure," he said, standing.

"Where are you going?" she asked, but he just gave her this cross between a wave and a salute, and walked away. He wasn't really walking so much as gliding, his feet in shadowy dress socks floating a couple of inches above the ground. "Wait, Uncle Luke," she said, because suddenly she wanted to tell him something—that it was all right, she didn't blame him for being a part of the web of secrecy and lies, she didn't even blame him for leaving without saying good-bye—she forgave him, it was okay, she understood. But as she gazed at his back, hunched over the way it had always been, as though he didn't think it was polite to be so tall, with the beautiful white Sunday dress shirt, she thought it would be corny and just plain wrong to say something like "I forgive you." And so instead she called, "Uncle Luke? Can I ask you something?"

He turned around.

"Did you know," she asked, "how much we would miss you?"

He seemed to think about this for a few seconds, a question that interested him. "I did," he said finally, meeting her gaze, "and I didn't." His blue eyes seemed amused and pleased with this answer. "I did, and I didn't," he repeated. "But now I do."

A slow, sad smile crept into his lips, into his eyes, one that made her throat ache. He turned around and glided toward the purple glass wall, and as he stepped through it, he began to fade, so that instead of ending up on the sidewalk, on the other side, he disappeared right into the dark glass. And then Audrey woke up, and found herself alone in the bus station, with nothing but the old canvas bag, and she felt a hollowness inside herself that was her uncle's absence and her being all alone in the station. It was loneliness. She just felt really lonely. But what was strange was that the loneliness felt bad, but not bad. It hurt, but it also felt good, like hunger before a big meal, or your mom brushing your hair too hard, or the ache in your legs from running when you were going really fast. It was like, she was lonely, but somehow it felt better than being not lonely.

Sleep

Luke is waging a war. The first week that he goes off his anti-depressants, he's an excited, wet-behind-the-ears recruit who feels good simply because he isn't experiencing any strange side effects and because he's buoyed by the excitement of battle. Then he awakens early one morning with a numbing pain throughout his body and the sinking belief that life is pointless and he's a loser and he really should go visit Mrs. Weiss in the hospital (stroke), but knows that he will not, and feels certain that he has been defeated. But later that afternoon at work, it's as though a morning fog has lifted and the sky is sunny and blue; he feels fine. He orders new books, prices two boxes of used ones, and arranges a display of Native American literature in the window in honor of Thanksgiving, all of which induces in him an immeasurable feeling of pride. *Take that.* The next night, he finds himself unable to sleep, unable to read, and spends six hours staring at the water stain on his stucco ceiling, until the first sunlight cracks through his bedroom window. For about a month, he feels perfectly normal. Christmas isn't easy—when has it been, since he was a boy?—but he suffers through it with the help of a week's supply of heavily spiked eggnog. Then, right after New Year's, he wakes up paralyzed. He can't get out of bed; he can't move his limbs. Terrified, he somehow manages to reach for the phone and call the one person who he knows won't take him to the hospital, the loony bin, who won't even tell their mother: Colleen. Still, it's a cry for help he can barely forgive himself.

It's been seven months now since he stopped taking anti-depressants, and he's a worn-out veteran who knows that it will always be like this. There will be no victor, no winner, no joy-ous environmentally incorrect ticker-tape parade, only the ebb and flow of battle, and in between, an uneasy truce. With invis-ible enemies. Confused motives. Poor morale. Jungle all around.

His mother wants to see him.

This is a nightmare, his worst fear coming true. His mother, Luke is certain, has somehow found out that he's depressed, that he's gone off his meds (whatever happened to doctor–client confidentiality?), and so has asked him to come to her office on Pacific Boulevard this morning. Luke drives there feeling car-sick. If he's right, and that's what this is about, then he has no idea what he'll do, what he'll say. Should he deny everything (Doctor who?), lie only partially (Yes, it's true, I saw a shrink, I took Prozac, Zoloft, MAO inhibitors, but it was only research for a book I'm writing, Mom), or come clean, and feel a strange combination (he imagines) of horror, increased nausea, and relief?

"Have a seat," his mother says.

Luke sits on the comfortable plush couch, while his mother sits behind her faux-antique Bombay Company desk. The room smells of fresh paint and virgin carpeting—it's in a brand-new Mediterranean villa of a minimall that his mother recently financed herself—and the toxic fumes are making him feel sick and disoriented, like an ant doused with Raid.

"What do you think of the grocery store?" she asks, making a steeple with her fingers under her chin.

At first Luke is confused, and then he understands: His mother is referring to the fine-food-and-wine shop on the second level, between the Thai pizza restaurant and the upscale home boutique, and is evidently going to broach the crisis of his clinical depression by making small talk. "I think it's great," he plays along. "San Pablo doesn't really have anything like that. I'm sure it'll be big."

She nods. "I think so too. That's why I was so pleased when I was talking to the owner, Frank DiCarlo, the other day, he's really a nice man, Luke, you're going to like him, and he told me he still hadn't found a manager, and I thought of you. He's based in San Francisco, see, and he needs someone reliable to run the store for him. When I told him that you managed a bookstore, and knew all about fine food and wine and all that, he was thrilled. He'll want to meet with you himself, of course, but I'm sure it's just a formality. We didn't talk numbers, but I'd guess the salary would be about twice what you're making now. So," she says, smiling, "what do you think?"

Luke is so relieved that he laughs, and his mother, clearly pleased by his reaction, laughs along with him. But then he gets ahold of himself and says, "No, Mother. I mean . . . no. No. No, thanks."

His mother briefly looks perplexed, but then the determined, savvy businesswoman recovers. "You think you'd be getting the job just because you're the developer's son. Let me tell you, that's not it at all. Maybe it helps, because Frank will know that he can trust you more than some Joe Schmo off the street, but it's you, your experience, that will land you the job. You'd be perfect."

Her last words echo in his mind. Perfect. He would be perfect. The perfect manager. The perfect manager of a fancy grocery store. He studies his mother's face. She's sixty-two, with a plumpish figure, short gray hair, and reading glasses that hang on a beaded chain around her neck, but she's still beautiful. Heroines in fairy tales are always said to have emerald eyes; his mother really does have them—eyes the color of emeralds, and the same smooth porcelain skin as Kate's, only his mother's is creased by two sharp lines on either side of her mouth. She was, what? thirty-three when his father died? He wonders if she had any suitors; perhaps she still does. Perhaps his mother has dated, engaged in love affairs; perhaps she's involved in one now, one with this nice Frank DiCarlo man, for example—what does Luke know?

"I know this might be hard for you to understand," he says, "but I like my job. I don't want to be manager of a big grocery store. I'm perfectly contented doing what I'm doing."

His mother nods, yet she looks sad, as though he were simply being stubborn, a little boy refusing to put on his coat.

"I know you have your . . . life-style," she says carefully. "I know you like your privacy." She bites her lip, and then the words come out in a rush: "Luke, I just want you to know, if you're gay, it doesn't make a bit of difference to me. Straight, gay, you're my son, and I want you to feel free to come out of the closet with me, do you understand?"

Luke might believe he didn't hear what he thought he heard if his mother didn't look so sincere. "Thanks, Mom," he finally says. "I appreciate it. I really do. But I'm not gay."

Despite her earlier proclamation, she appears relieved. "Oh," she says. "Well, then."

"I don't see what my sexual preference has to do with my preference for work."

"But is this really your preference? Money isn't everything," she adds, before he can respond. "I know that. But don't you want a new challenge? Greater responsibilities? I guess what I'm asking you is, Are you sure that you're living up to your potential? Forget about the grocery store for a minute," she says, waving her hand. "You're thirty-six. Think about it, Luke. Thirty-six. Isn't it time for you to decide what you really want to do with your life? For you to make something of yourself? You have a degree from a good college. You could be anything—a journalist, a professor, an advertising executive. Don't laugh, it can be very creative work. A screenwriter, then. Or a teacher."

"Mom—"

"Luke, angel." She reaches across the desk until her hands curl over the edge. "What about a family? Don't you want to get married, have kids?"

Luke tries not to smile. A wife, intimacy, a job as the manager of an upscale grocery store, a couple of kids . . . His mother might as well be asking him if he wouldn't like to be abducted by big-eyed aliens who will take him, warp speed, to their galaxy in an oval spaceship. He's been off psychotropic drugs for seven months and he's still more or less able to function. This is his accomplishment. His victory.

He gazes at his mother's face, filled with maternal anxiety and concern, and contemplates what he can say to satisfy her, to explain.

"Maybe I just haven't met the right woman yet."

His mom looks at him, and slowly smiles; this is the right answer, a clichéd response that implies optimism and hope. "Oh, Luke honey," she says. "You will."

All day the bright, sunny light has been oppressive, like a happy face when you're not, and Luke decides to close the bookstore early and go home. It isn't even five yet, and it's a Tuesday, when Jerry's always stays open until eight to accommodate the after-work crowd, but guess what? Luke closes the bookstore at eight, or five, or four-forty, and the earth still spins on its axis around the sun.

He flips the sign on the glass door to "Closed," walks to the parking lot behind the store, and gets into his Toyota. He's driving to his apartment when he finds himself continuing straight on Harbor instead of turning right on Sixth. This sudden, inexplicable action is so unlike him (he's always been, as Colleen once half-jokingly put it, about as spontaneous as a rock) that even he's curious where he's heading, a surprised passenger being taken for a Sunday drive. He comes to the end of Harbor, turns right onto Vista del Mar, drives for a mile or so, believing now that he'll simply make a loop—right on Pacific, and right again on Sixth—to go to his apartment, when he comes to the gravel lot above the beach, and turns in. He steps outside, breathes in the salty, breezy air, and sits on the warm hood of his car.

The beach is sheltered by craggy cliffs on either side. To the left, beyond the peninsula, is the harbor; to the right, just up the road, beyond the new Venetian condominium complex, and across from the eucalyptus tree, is where his father died. For an instant, he can vividly see it all: shattered glass, the crashed car, his father's body, bloody and limp, his father the same age Luke is now, the drunk driver staggering away. The realization that this is where it happened gives Luke a strange feeling, something akin to longing. He seldom thinks about his father, hardly remembers him (he's been dead for most of Luke's life, after all), but maybe this strange, unfamiliar feeling is his missing him. Maybe he misses his dad.

He gazes at the vivid orange sun, the indigo sea, the sand dotted with stragglers. If his father could see him now, Luke thinks, he probably wouldn't like what he saw. He'd consider him a failure, of course, just as his mother does. He's melancholic, introverted, overly serious, not the kind of son you'd take to football games or construction sites or raucous bars to knock back shots and play pool. Novels and poetry, like religion, are for women and children, and there's something not quite right about a grown man who has built his life around reading, buying, and selling books, Luke is sure his father would believe. As for his melancholia or clinical depression or whatever the hell it is, why can't Luke just pull himself out of it?

He walks to the edge of the cliff and looks down. White foam swirls around the jutting rocks. The ocean is endless, and deep. The roar of the waves crashing on the lethal rocks vibrates in his ears. It would be easy to step off. To fall, and keep falling, and die quickly of a broken neck, so that he wouldn't even know he was dead. To never feel pain, never, ever again. To never experience another moment like this—when the blue ocean and sky, the black cliffs strewn with soft white California buckwheat, even the seagull squawking overhead, all mock him, show him how small and unbeautiful he is.

He takes a step forward, and then stops, because an image has come into his mind, unwanted and unsummoned, of his mother. *I brought you into this world,* he imagines her saying, *and Goddamnit you'd better not take yourself out of it.* His courage or fear or whatever it is begins to waver, and the spell is broken. He sees not an end to his own pain, but his mother's angry face looming over his casket.

He shivers in the warm air. Then he walks to his car, curls inside, and drives home. It was just another battle, and he isn't sure whether he's lost or won.

Luke can't move. He can see his long, ugly feet, with their hairy toes, dangling off the edge of the bed, exposed by the sheet that reaches only to his ankles, and his pale hands, one of which rests on his stomach, while the other lies on the bed beside his thigh, but whatever mechanism is supposed to send a message from his brain to his limbs is on the fritz. Panic rises in the center of his chest, a bird flapping its wings. Luke inhales deeply, then exhales, having learned from experience (this has happened a number of times since he first awakened to find himself paralyzed, and called Colleen) that the most important thing is to remain calm.

First, he blinks rapidly, opens and closes his jaw, moves his head from side to side, and sucks his stomach in and out, making use of the muscles over which he has control to wake his body up. Then he concentrates on wiggling his fingers and toes. Nothing happens. He concentrates harder, summoning all his will, and watches his fingers wiggle up and down. Good. Now he closes his eyes, and imagines himself rolling onto his side, pushing his torso up, his legs falling naturally to the floor. (This visualization technique is something he appropriated from a book called *Inner Skiing,* which Jerry absolutely swears by, in which you imagine yourself skiing gracefully over moguls as you go up the chairlift before each run.) He starts over and imagines the scenario again, and again, until he feels sure that he's ready, and then, without thinking about it at all (that's the trick at this stage, he's learned), he opens his eyes, rolls onto his side, and pushes his torso off the bed.

Now that the initial movement is over, everything else—standing, walking—comes easily. He goes to the bathroom. He feeds Rosie (the little Manx he adopted after Mrs. Weiss went into the nursing home—he needs a cat like he needs a killer whale, but Mrs. Weiss called him on the phone and asked him, so what could he do?), cleans her litter box, changes her bowl of water. He makes himself a cup of instant coffee, which he drinks black, takes a few sips of orange juice directly from the carton. Then he goes back to bed.

In the afternoon, the telephone rings.

"Hello?"

"Uncle Luke. Where are you? I mean, I know you're home, but why?"

It's the Fourth of July. He's supposed to spend the day with his family at the beach, and then go to Alek's house for a barbecue.

Luke imagines the barbecue on the balcony of Alek's perfect little beach *casa*—with the fancy food, the decent wine, the humorous anecdotes about faculty politics or some intriguing story about Alek's family back in Mexico and El Paso; he imagines trying to engage in the holiday festivities—the fireworks, the sparklers, the laughter—and it's like facing the prospect of walking the length of North America: No can do.

"I'm not feeling all that well," Luke says. "A touch of the flu, I'm afraid."

"In July?"

"Maybe it's just a cold. A summer cold. You know, those are often worse than winter ones." He hopes Audrey buys the folksy wisdom.

"That's too bad. Alek's making seafood shish kebabs and basmati rice."

"I'm not at all hungry," he says, which is true. He hasn't been hungry for days, weeks, maybe even years.

"Do you want us to bring you anything?"

"No," Luke replies, more vehemently than he intended. "I mean, I don't need a thing. You enjoy yourselves. I just need some rest, all right?"

"Uncle Luke?" Audrey says, very softly. "You're not really sick, are you?"

The silence between them is tense, like the silence in a courtroom before a verdict.

"Are you?"

"No, I'm not," Luke says. Then he adds, "I've never been a big fireworks fan, and I suppose I just feel like staying in tonight."

"It's all right, Uncle Luke."

"You won't tell anyone else, will you? It's just . . . I'm not sure they'd understand."

"I'll tell them you have a cold. A summer cold. Grandma will say, 'Poor Luke. Those are harder to shake than winter ones.' I'll tell her you're getting some rest."

Luke scratches Rosie behind the ears. She gives him a grateful look and purrs into his thigh.

"I'd appreciate it."

"Well, have a good night."

"You too."

He turns off the phone, tells himself he'll have to be more careful.

"What's the matter?" his mother asks him.

Luke sets down his fork. "What do you mean?"

She points to his full plate. "You've barely touched your food. I thought you loved chicken curry."

His mother has made two curry dishes this evening—chicken and sweet potatoes, whose spicy, complex flavors he usually enjoys—but he realizes now that he's been chewing, swallowing, sipping Tsingtao, and finally, pushing food around on his plate, without having tasted a thing.

"I suppose I'm just hot."

"It is kind of hot to be eating curry, Mom," Kate says. "Maybe we should have made a tossed salad."

Alek laughs. "I'm sorry, but grown men and thirteen-year-old runners can't make a meal out of tossed salad. Mary, this is delicious, believe me."

A tingle of annoyance at this remark by Kate's perfect diplomat of a boyfriend creeps over Luke's skin, and disappears. The truth is, Luke is grateful to Alek, deeply grateful, for filling in, putting the spotlight on himself, making it easier for Luke to fade into the background. Sometimes he can go an entire Friday evening saying barely a word.

"I'm glad *you're* enjoying it," his mother says, as though Alek were the only one who mattered, since he's the only one grateful enough to heartily eat the dinner she's prepared. She turns to Luke and says, "If you're hot, why don't you turn up the AC?"

"Maybe I will," Luke answers, not because it's all that warm inside, but because once you've made up a story, you have to stick with it. He turns the thermostat down several degrees, sits at the table again, and forces himself to eat every tasteless bite on his plate.

One day in August, Kate stops by the bookstore at noon and asks if he wants to go to lunch.

"Lunch?" Luke repeats. Since he lost his sense of taste, he's had less appetite than ever and no interest in eating, and he often works through the lunch hour.

"Yeah, you know, that meal some people eat at this time of day? Have you had breakfast yet?"

Luke shakes his head.

"Neither have I. Let's go to the diner and we can have breakfast instead."

Kate, who never eats before noon, loves oatmeal and omelets and whole-grain waffles, and her eyes light up as she says the word "diner." It would be too awkward if Luke were to say no (he can't think of an excuse, anyway), and so he puts the "Closed" sign on the door, and locks up.

As they walk the block and a half to the diner, Kate talks about an idea she has for a new project, something about Zeus swallowing a fly that turns into Athena, that's going to be about Kate and Audrey, but Luke isn't paying much attention, because he has to concentrate on the task of putting one foot in front of the other quickly, as quickly as his sister, in the dank heat.

They sit at a booth in the air-conditioned diner, order, and then Kate says, "A weird thing happened a couple weeks ago." She pauses to sip her iced coffee. "I thought I was pregnant."

Her words could be coming from underwater. Luke has to translate for himself what she said, and then think of an appropriate way to respond. He's still thinking as Kate goes on.

"Of course I thought, 'Oh great, my daughter's thirteen and I'm pregnant?' But beyond the fear and nervousness, there was something like excitement. And that really surprised me."

It occurs to Luke to ask, "What did Alek say?"

"Are you crazy? If I told him I was one day late for my period he'd be out buying cribs and making lists of possible names. I would never tell him unless I was sure. Then a few days ago, this kid he coaches at the Boys Club got into an accident, and it turns out he might be paralyzed from the waist down. Oh God, it's so awful. Now Alek goes to the hospital every afternoon, and he's thinking about organizing a basketball team for kids in wheelchairs. I mean, he would make such a great father, is it really fair that I stay with him if I don't want to have more children? Or if I don't want to marry him? And you know, I really don't understand why I don't want these things." She lets out a sigh. "Listen to me. I'm blathering."

Luke feels the way he does whenever he sits beside Audrey on his mother's couch, watching TV with the sound turned off. She flips through channels, pausing at sitcoms and commercials and police dramas only long enough for Luke to observe the silent antics, sales pitches, and intense interrogations for the chimeras they are, feeling completely uninvolved, before she moves on to something else. He stares at his sister's face, which he's often thought has the odd, quiet beauty of a painting that becomes more interesting the longer you study it, but now she's one-dimensional, flat, almost grainy to him. He glances around the diner, which also has a surface like a TV screen. Everything is flat, gray, alien.

"I'm sorry," she tells him. "I didn't mean to use you as a sounding board."

"No, it's all right," Luke says.

"I guess I haven't really had anyone to talk to about this. I mean, I couldn't tell Alek, and Mom . . . forget it. But enough about me," she says. "What's going on with you?"

Luke is saved by the arrival of their food. He dodges the question by arranging his silverware and napkin, sprinkling salt and pepper, and finally offering, "Tell me more about your new project."

"Oh God, you don't want to hear about that."

"I do, I really do."

"Okay, well. I'm not quite finished with the Medusa I've been working on yet. But I was thinking that . . ."

As Kate talks, Luke feels he's there, but not there. A part of him listens well enough to ask questions that enable her to continue talking, while another part of him observes the whole thing from a distance. It's this part of him, the part that isn't really there, that is the most real to Luke. And it's then, as this other self listens to Kate talk, and watches the embodied Luke nod and shovel tasteless food into his mouth, that he feels a sharp tremor in the back of his throat, and reaches for his glass of water. The clear liquid tastes like cotton, like wood; it's sticky and fibrous, difficult to swallow. He sucks an ice cube into his mouth and lets it melt on his tongue. The resulting coolness washes him with something like calm. He sets down the glass and looks at Kate, afraid that she's sensed something, but she's blithely drizzling maple syrup over her pancakes, talking away. ". . . because the longer I imagined that headache—I mean, just imagine, giving birth out of your head?—the more I thought it was the perfect metaphor . . ." It seems impossible, but there it is: His sister hasn't noticed a thing.

Luke can no longer remember when the bad days began to out-number the good, when the good ones became grounds for celebration just because he didn't feel like weeping the moment he woke up; in fact, he can no longer remember the last good day he had, and has no reason to think he will ever have a good day again. He calls in sick to work more and more often (the part-timer doesn't mind; he can use the extra hours to pay for his Corvette), and spends the days lying in bed, unable to move, unable to sleep, experiencing a gray pain in every cell of his body, thinking how nice it would be to be dead, how pleasant, how utterly satisfying, like a trip to the Fiji islands, but wondering who in the world has the energy and strength to actually concoct and carry out such a plan?

And then one morning in late September, he awakens feeling: all right. Not like the sun is shining and the birds are chirping (though they are, of course, they are), but not terrible. Not bad. His bedroom is a mess, and he tidies it up a little before he goes to work. At the bookstore, he does inventory, tends to a few things he's fallen behind on, makes sure everything's in order. He's feeling better now. Almost good. Not good enough to live until he has a heart attack at eighty-five, but good enough to kill himself. Good enough to die.

He's been thinking of death for so long—the idea of pure nothingness waiting for him on the other side has been his constant, comforting companion these past few months—that to realize he's going to send himself there, and soon, makes him feel a sharpness and clarity he hasn't experienced in years. He paces around the bookstore, not really thinking so much as enjoying the once familiar hum of his brain, calm, restful, released. The knowledge that the cold wet drizzle that is his life will soon be over makes him feel—there's only one word for it, and the irony isn't lost on him—alive. For the first time in eons, it seems, he feels alive.

A gun is out of the question. He doesn't own one, has never held one or even seen one, except on TV, and he's afraid he might miss something vital and instead of dying merely give himself permanent brain damage. He imagines his mother coming to see him in the hospital every day, her son the vegetable, the suicide manqué. No, thank you. Besides, he's read stories about people who blow their brains out, and he knows that whoever finds him would have to scrape things off the wall, things like tissue and bone, and he doesn't want his brains on a wall, or anyone having to scrape them off. No, shooting himself would be a last, unmistakable cry of "Fuck you," whereas he wants his last action to convey a message closer to: "Sorry, I tried, I really did, but, well, I just can't."

He thinks about rope—hanging seems a quick, certain, almost elegant method—but there's nothing to hang himself from in his apartment. Carbon monoxide is out as well: his building doesn't have a garage, and he isn't about to stick his head in an oven, Plath-like, because it seems too absurd, too loaded with issues of feminism and the Holocaust, and because he doesn't want anything to happen to Rosie. That leaves pills. He goes to the clinic, complains about insomnia to a doctor he's never met, and gets a prescription for Seconal. Pills and booze. The lethal combination makes him think of rock musicians in trashed hotel rooms, not Luke Patrick Flannigan, son of sturdy midwesterners Grady and Mary, brother to Kate and Colleen, uncle to Audrey, Jennifer, and Ryan, loyal bookstore manager extraordinaire. But it will have to do.

There's one moment, while he's sitting on the back deck at his mother's—it's a Friday in early October, the air is fresh and cool, and she comes up behind him and puts her hand on his shoulder (just her hand, just setting it there, but his mother has never been a physically demonstrative person)—when he thinks, Maybe I won't go through with it. Maybe I'll get help. Maybe I'll tell her, right now: Mom, I need help.

"Mom?" Luke says.

"Yes, angel."

The vision of his life after those loaded, weighty words comes to him in only a second or two of time, but he sees it all:

the struggle with more antidepressants and their hopeless side effects, the hospitalization for depression, the group rap sessions, the electroshock therapy, the years spread out like desert sand, empty and dry and without end.

"Nothing."

"What were you going to say?"

She takes her hand away; the absence of her hand on his shoulder feels like a presence, like a weight. A familiar sensation, as though he's felt that absence all his life.

"The coq au vin you made tonight. It was very good."

"Really?"

Luke ate everything on his plate without tasting a thing, but he looks into his mother's beautiful, pleased eyes, and nods.

"Delicious."

"It wasn't too dry?"

"It was perfect."

"Well." She smiles at him. "Thank you, honey," she says.

For quite some time now, he writes on the top sheet of a yellow legal pad, and then pauses. He likes the beginning—it's historical, chronological, pseudoscientific—but how to go on? *I have not felt quite like myself.* That's ridiculous: he has felt much too much like himself. He crosses it out. *I have felt a strange numbness in my brain, a pain inside myself that, if physical, would certainly have put my body into some state of shock.* That doesn't begin to get at it—So go into shock, his mother would respond—and he crosses that out as well. What can he possibly say? Good-bye, cruel world? It isn't your fault? I can't go on? All of these lamentations have a darkly humorous aura. He sets down his pen. If he could write a suicide note, then perhaps he would have been able to communicate to someone his pain, that is, perhaps he would have been able to put the ineffable into words, and he wouldn't need to kill himself. This is a revelation, and he scribbles: *If I could write a suicide note, I wouldn't need to die. Therefore, good-bye.* He writes this feeling certain he's captured exactly what he needs to say, but when he reads it over, he's as amazed as if he'd written in a language he never learned. It's a ditty, a nursery rhyme; in another place and time, it would make him laugh out loud. He rips the sheet from the pad, crumples it into a ball, and throws it into the wastebasket.

It's sunny but not too warm, a perfect day to mow the lawn. Luke pushes the mower to the far edge of the grass, pulls the cord only once before it catches—a minor miracle, which makes him feel lucky and pleased—and walks in a straight line, from the far edge, just in front of the towering pine, to the deck (careful around the sinuous bed of no-care portulaca and the jacaranda against the fence), before curving the mower around and beginning a second row. It's an old gas mower, ancient, but—except for when Luke was in college and his sisters filled in for him the weekends he didn't come home—Luke has used this mower for most of his life, and he has always been rather alarmed when his mother talks about getting a new model, something easier to use. He's always dissuaded her by saying he needs the exercise, but the fact is, he's nostalgic about this old object, and the aches in his shoulders and stooped back are well worth the satisfaction he feels pushing the pitiful rusting thing.

He begins a third row and finds himself humming "Whistle While You Work." He's forgotten how much he used to enjoy this task. For years, it's been nothing more than a filial responsibility, a duty, a job he's continued to do simply because he's always done it. But as a child, he loved the grown-up sensations of pushing the mower with his skinny arms, of setting out the bags of green waste, right along with Mr. Thompson from across the street and Mr. Brown from next door, feeling a manly surge of pride. Even when he was in high school he enjoyed the ritual, though by that time it was more for the adultish satisfactions of attention to detail and a job well done, of gazing on a short, neat, evenly cut lawn. He remembers these old feelings of pleasure as he makes a curve in front of the rubber tree, careful around the protruding roots, then pushes the mower in a straight line toward the house, breathing in the freshly cut grass.

He wonders who will tend his mother's lawn when he's gone. The idea of Alek's doing it makes him feel territorial. He can just see him out here with some high-powered mower, cutting the grass, raking leaves, undoubtedly even planting perennials and shrubs. But so what? What's it to him? Let Alek plant flowers and shrubs—let him install some marble fountain with a cherub spewing water out of its open fishlike mouth—what does Luke care? He won't be around.

He switches off the mower, pushes it to the side of the house toward the front lawn—much smaller, an easy, five-minute task—and hears: "Uncle Luke."

He turns around. Audrey's sitting on the shaded porch, in shorts and a T-shirt, smiling at him.

"Where'd you come from?" Luke asks, and then notices Kate's Volvo wagon parked in the driveway behind his Toyota. "When did you get here?"

"Just now. Mom's inside with Grandma, but I wanted to stay out here for a while. It's so nice, isn't it?"

"Beautiful."

Audrey studies his face. "You look different."

"I do?"

"Yeah, you look . . . I don't know. Well rested or something. Or like maybe you've been getting some sun. Not that that's supposed to be good for you . . ."

"I got a trim."

"No, that's not it. You just look . . . different."

"I feel different," Luke says, a bit recklessly.

"Really? How?"

He smiles at her. "Just . . . different."

Instead of laughing, she frowns. "I know what you mean. I've been feeling different too. It's kind of scary, isn't it?"

Luke wipes his forehead with his sleeve and stares at his niece's fresh, lovely face. He almost regrets that he won't be around to know what kind of person she'll become—she might very well be quite fascinating—but then he tells himself that probably all young people are interesting before they become run-of-the-mill adults, and besides, he simply can't wait. Still, he wants to give her something, some recognition—no, some knowledge of herself—and so he says, "When you were little, and I used to take you to the park, you used to swing so high, do you remember?"

She nods. "I loved to swing."

"Sometimes it would frighten me. I thought you might swing right over the bar." He shakes his head. "I've always admired your . . . bravery."

She meets his eyes, a skeptical expression on her face.

"I've got to mow the front now," he tells her.

He pushes the mower onto the grass, pulls the cord a couple of times until it catches, and begins to mow.

Luke goes to his desk, slips out a sheet of paper, and writes his will. He leaves his little Manx cat to Audrey and his CD player to his mother, who doesn't have one. The four five-piece place settings of Russel Wright Iroquois Casual dishes he found at a garage sale he leaves to Kate, who always admired them. To Colleen, he leaves his 1987 Toyota Corolla, because the brakes are going and the clutch sometimes sticks, and he figures that Sam will be able to fix it. He leaves Jennifer and Ryan his two favorite novels from childhood, the only ones he's kept— *Treasure Island* and *Alice in Wonderland*—and wills the rest of his books to Jerry. He leaves his mother all his stocks, of course, and writes her a check for sixteen hundred dollars, which is all the money he has in the bank, in hopes it will cover the funeral expenses.

Then he sits down with the books he brought home from

work and finds out how many Seconal it will take to do the trick.

One last item of business: He picks up the cordless phone his mother gave him last Christmas and presses Memory 1.

"Hello."

"Mom?" Luke says. "Did I wake you?"

"Wake me? It's eight-fifteen. I might be getting old, but I'm not dead. What's up?"

"I couldn't find Colleen's number."

She rattles off the number, which he also knows by heart, and besides has stored in the phone's memory. "Don't forget they're an hour ahead," she says.

"I won't."

"And it's a school night, though God knows, those kids stay up late enough."

"I won't call too late. Mom?"

"Hmm?"

"I just wanted you to know. You've been a good mother to me. To all of us. It hasn't . . . it hasn't been your fault. Nothing has. Not at all. I just wanted you to know that."

His mother's television hums in the background. "Luke, honey, are you all right? What in the world are you talking about?"

"I'm just telling you . . ." he begins. Why are these words so hard to say? "I'm just telling you, Mom, that I love you."

There's a short pause, and his mother answers, "I love you too."

"I know you do, Mom."

"Luke, angel. Are you sure you're all right?"

"Positive. Everything's great. Really. I just wanted you to know that."

"Well, I appreciate it. I do."

"I'm gonna go now, Mom. I'll see you. Okay?"

"Luke?"

"Yes?"

"Nothing, honey. Good night."

Luke hangs up before she can say anything else. He doesn't feel sad, or sorry, or worried, he feels—well, he doesn't feel anything, really. He's completed a task. He's told his mother he loves her, and has given her the opportunity to say the same to him, thereby freeing her from any absurd, misplaced sense of guilt she might feel after his death.

Once upon a time, thinking of her would have stopped him, but he's beyond that now. He's no longer that person. He's been taken over: by a gray absence, or a Luke different from anyone he's known, or maybe they're the same thing. His blood and ligaments and heart and toes throb with a dull, terrible pain every time he moves, every time he breathes, every second of his fitful sleep.

He can't feel sorry for his mother; he can't even feel sorry for himself. He's become a mindless organism requiring an end to its own suffering. That's all.

Luke awakens early the following morning with an unearthly sense of peace. It's his day off. He walks to a nearby café, orders a cappuccino, and sits at a table in a corner, away from the window, observing the people around him. Two men in yellow construction helmets are eating elephant ears; a guy with a shaved head is reading *The Economist*; and two women at the table next to Luke's bend toward each other, speaking in hushed voices. Luke, who can't remember the last time he felt a thread of curiosity and interest, gazes at them in awe over their friendship, their intimacy, wondering what they're talking about with such intensity. It strikes him that he could go to their table and introduce himself. He pictures himself sitting next to them, his head forward, engrossed, and becoming a part of their intriguing conversation, perhaps even their lives. Of course he would never do it. But the very idea leaves what feels like the glimmer of a smile on his mouth. He takes a last sip of his drink, goes to the counter, and puts a twenty-dollar bill into the tip jar before he walks outside.

On his way home, Luke sees a white dress shirt in the window of a men's shop. He pauses on the sidewalk, admiring its crispness and clean lines, then enters the store and buys it, and a new pair of socks as well. He spends the afternoon tidying his apartment, playing with his cat, and preparing the dinner he decided on with some care. He grills two salmon steaks on the balcony (one for him and one for Rosie), steams some jasmine rice, roasts a few baby carrots with rosemary, and makes a salad of tomatoes, mozzarella, and fresh basil.

He sits down to his dinner with a glass of Beaujolais, and proceeds to eat slowly, savoring each bite. The salmon is succulent, exquisite; it just about melts in his mouth. The fish contrasts nicely with the sharpness of the rosemary, which in turn is complemented by the mellow jasmine rice. The wine is soft, slightly fruity without being downright sweet, light-bodied, delicious. It's all an illusion, of course. The pleasure of this supper lies entirely in the knowledge that it's his last, that he will never bring another bite of food into his mouth again, that he won't need to. Still, he enjoys the meal more than he can remember enjoying anything in some time. He eats the salad last, with a little olive oil and balsamic vinegar, and tops everything off with pistachio ice cream. He washes the dishes, dries them, and puts them away.

After a few minutes of standing in his little kitchen, staring at his old gas stove, the burn ring on the wooden counter, the cheap linoleum floor with the faded red-wine stain by the fridge, sad familiar props of a play in which he'll never act again, he goes to the living room and calls his landlord. He wants a mere acquaintance to find his body, so he tells Mr. Hernandez that his sink is clogged and asks him to come fix it in the morning. Then, as though preparing for a fine occasion—a wedding, perhaps his own—he takes a long, hot shower, after which he stands in front of the mirror with a towel around his waist, ready to shave. He wipes the foggy mirror with his hand, and sees his destiny: eyes circled by dark rings; white, ghostly skin; a sullen, hunched back—it's his shadow, the little boy, gazing at him with an unmistakable smirk. *I've won,* say his victorious, curled-up lips, his gloating eyes. *You've lost. Poor Luke. Too bad.*

And then the hallucination vanishes; the shadow is gone. The boy's dark eyes are replaced by Luke's blue ones, his coal-black hair by Luke's dishwater blond. But that haggard, pale skin, the dark circles around the eyes, the old man's posture: they're the same.

"Aren't you handsome?" he whispers.

He shaves carefully, methodically, and splashes on the after-shave Kate gave him for his last birthday, which he's never bothered to open until now. Finally he puts on his most comfortable khakis and his new shirt and socks.

Groomed and dressed, he goes into the living room and stands in front of his stereo. His favorite pieces of music are Bach's Brandenburg Concertos, but they've always made him sad. He's not sure he wants to feel sad just before he dies. He decides on a Mozart sonata.

He takes his sleeping pills slowly, with the rest of the bottle of wine. Then he lies on the couch, listening to the music. He stares at the ceiling, and waits, and it seems to him that time is slowing down. He sees his entire life pass before his eyes—not flashing, like a quick snapshot, but lingering, like a slow, decades-long movie. He tastes the banana-rum cake his mother made last Christmas Eve, and the mildly bittersweet flavor of its decorative poinsettias; he sees Dr. Vernor, with his warm eyes and thick beard; he gazes upon the sad expression of the older woman who came into the bookstore years before, and feels the surprising coolness of her beautiful hands when he places the change in her palm; he's walking across campus after an English class when it occurs to him that, with each step, he's moving into a future filled with beauty, and art, and endless possibilities; he's riding his skateboard down a hill with Tommy Lanz, and they're going much too fast—the board is trembling beneath him and the wind is rushing in his ears, and any second now he'll leave the earth and sail into the air. Then he sees his father, in distinct detail—his enormous height, his broad, strong shoulders, his huge hands with their amazingly gentle touch—and hears the sound of the floorboards creak as his father bends to kiss him good night (Luke is in the softest bed, with the cleanest sheets), and he can smell the aftershave, sweat, and tobacco that is his father's scent, and his father's face is coming closer, and closer, and Luke wants to stay awake to feel his father's lips on his cheek, but he's so sleepy, so sleepy, and his father's eyes seem to say to him, *It's all right, I know you're tired, son, it's all right,* and Luke knows that everything is going to be okay, that everything is fine now, and he closes his eyes, and falls asleep.

Self-Portrait with Ghosts

Kate awakened at three in the morning to a dry melancholy, as though she was lacking something, a lover who was supposed to have been beside her, perhaps, or a limb. She sat up in bed, looked around the dark room, and realized what it was: Luke. Luke wasn't sitting at the foot of her bed, expectant and slightly amused. He wasn't standing in front of the window, peering out. Or rather, she wasn't imagining him beside her, doing these things, which meant . . . what? That she no longer needed to imagine him beside her? That it was time to begin letting him go? Maybe she was just too sleepy.

She thought of Audrey, of their little talk, and decided that the worst was behind them. They would never be over Luke's suicide—of course not, it was something all of them would carry around every day, every hour, wherever they went—but maybe they could learn to live with it, just as, perhaps, she and Audrey could come to a closer understanding. Nothing was hidden between them anymore, no big secrets, no half-truths, no—why not admit it?—lies.

Kate slipped into her bathrobe (buttery soft, silk, olive

green, a present from Alek) and walked down the hall in her bare feet. She turned the knob on Audrey's door slowly, so that she wouldn't wake her, and glanced inside. But what she saw didn't make any sense (she was tired, it was dark), and so she stepped closer. She went all the way to the bed and still couldn't trust her sight; she patted the covers and mattress to make sure. But it was true: Audrey wasn't there.

Her legs felt weak and shaky, and she sat on the bed. She stared at the closet, which was open only a crack, and it occurred to her that Audrey might be in there right now, teaching her a lesson, enjoying the terror undoubtedly all over her face. She stood up, turned on the overhead light, and opened the closet door. Audrey hadn't brought a lot of clothes to her grandmother's, and half of those she had brought were gone. Kate turned around and searched the bed for what she knew would be the telltale sign: Audrey's stuffed polar bear, Paw-Paw, with the missing eye and falling-apart seams, which Luke had given her when she and Sam had gotten divorced, and which Audrey had never, ever, not even when they'd gone camping or to Mexico, slept without.

Kate hurried back to her room, reached for the phone, and called Alek.

"Hello," he managed to say.

"Alek, I need you to wake up right now."

"Jesus, Kate, what is it?"

"Audrey's gone."

"What do you mean, gone?"

"I mean she isn't in her bed and half of her clothes are missing."

"I'll be right over. Kate?"

"What?"

"It's going to be okay. I know it will."

"Hurry," she said, and hung up the phone.

Audrey is fine, she told herself. This is a nightmare, this is a dream. I'm going to wake up any minute.

She went downstairs, unlocked the door and turned on the porch light for Alek, then walked toward her mother's study. The door was closed, but the light was still on. Her mom had probably fallen asleep there once again, on the futon, in her clothes, her reading glasses still on the chain around her neck. Her mother. The news that Audrey had disappeared, run away from home with her ratty stuffed bear, would tear whatever shred of heart her mother had left into a thousand pieces. Or no. Maybe she didn't even have a shred of heart left. Maybe she would take the news of her granddaughter's disappearance with stony equanimity. Maybe she would look at Kate as if to say, "So? What else do you expect from this life?"

In the kitchen Kate took out a flashlight from the utility drawer. She searched the family room, where Rosie half opened her eyes and blinked from her perch atop the couch, and the living room, and even the downstairs bathroom, because maybe Audrey was playing an elaborate game of hide-and-seek, maybe she'd taken her clothes and bear with her to worry Kate, to scare her to death. It was Halloween, wasn't it? Yes, maybe this was just some misguided Halloween prank. She stepped onto the deck. "Audrey?" she called, shining the light on trees, shrubs, the long grass.

Nothing was out there, not even a cat, not even a sound. She went back inside. She grabbed her mom's address book from the kitchen counter and went upstairs, into her room, and reached for the phone.

"Yeah."

Kate was startled by the familiarity of that groggy voice. "Sam, this is Kate."

"Kate?" he repeated. "What . . . what is it?"

"Listen, I'm sorry to wake you, but I was wondering if you'd heard from Audrey."

"It's Kate," he said, away from the phone, and then into it: "Audrey? No, I haven't heard from her. Why? What's going on?"

"We had a little fight last night. To tell you the truth, it was kind of about you, and tonight she isn't in her bed, and I thought that maybe . . . she might have gone to see you."

"To see me?"

"Well, it's a possibility."

"She isn't in her bed, huh?"

"No."

"Jeez, Kate, I don't know what to say. She hasn't come here. When was the last time you saw her?"

"Just before eleven tonight."

"When?" she heard Colleen say, and Sam told her, "Just before eleven tonight," and then Colleen said something else, and Sam told Kate, "Yeah, she wouldn't be here yet if she got a ride or something. Is there anywhere else she might have gone?"

Kate let out a deep breath. "I don't know."

"Do you think she might have slipped out to go meet her friends? Maybe even . . . you know. A boyfriend?"

Kate thought she might cry, the idea made her feel so relieved. Everything she'd feared, everything she'd preached against, railed about, she hoped to God Audrey was doing right now: partying, drinking beer, smoking pot, making out with some pimply sixteen-year-old in the backseat of a car. Perhaps she'd gone to some boyfriend's house for the weekend, and that's why she'd packed a bag, that's why she'd taken Paw-Paw with her, because she was so young, so young, she didn't understand that you couldn't sleep with your arms around a lover and a stuffed bear both at once. Audrey could come home pregnant and Kate wouldn't care—she would raise the two of them together, daughter and grandchild, never letting either out of her sight.

"Sorry I woke you," Kate told him, embarrassed now. "I'll call you later, okay?"

"No, don't hang up. Hey. Is there anything you need for us to do?"

"Please, no. I'm sorry. I'm going to call her best friend now. Maybe she'll know where Audrey is."

But Sandira hadn't heard from her, hadn't seen her, didn't know about any boyfriend, had no idea where in the world Audrey might be.

"Maybe she went for a run," she said, with the logic of someone roused at three in the morning.

Audrey's running shoes were still in her closet, and nobody went for a run carrying around a bunch of clothes in the middle of the night, but what Kate said was, "Sandira, I know how hard it is to betray a friend's trust, and I wouldn't ask you to do it if it weren't really important. But I need to ask you to be truthful with me. This is an emergency."

"I'm sorry, Miz Flannigan," Sandira said. "I mean, I don't know what I'd tell you if Audrey swore me to secrecy or something, but she didn't. She didn't say a word to me about anything. I mean, stick a zillion needles in my eye and all that, I honestly don't know where she is."

Alek hugged her hard when she met him on the porch, pressing his cheek against hers, holding her as if trying to receive and offer comfort at the same time.

"I don't know what I'll do if we can't find—"

"Shhh," he said, and broke away, her face between his hands. "We're gonna find her, whatever it takes," he said, a promise, a threat, a demand. And Kate believed him. Of course she did. What choice did she have?

San Pablo was smaller than a city, bigger than a town, and every square foot of it was a place where Audrey might have been, and then a place where she was not. Kate and Alek went to the lookout above the oceanside cliffs, down to the beach, to the running trail along Vista del Mar. They checked Denny's, CoCo's, and Taco Bell (the only restaurants still open), and then drove to Cypress Street, where, Alek said, there was supposed to have been a high school Halloween party that night.

Beer bottles dotted the lawn; a few cars were parked along the curb. They walked around the side of the house to the back-yard, and Kate could feel her expectations surge along with her pulse when she saw the group of kids in the hot tub—naked, or at least topless, wielding bottles of beer—but none was close to being Audrey.

"Mr. Perez," one of them said, and they all looked nervous and embarrassed, as though they'd been spotted, half naked and drunk, by the cops.

"Do any of you know if Audrey Flannigan was here tonight?" he asked.

"Audrey who?"

"The runner."

"Don't know her."

"Yeah, she was one of the vampires."

"No, that was Lexy and Elaine."

"I know her," a male voice said. The boy wasn't in the hot tub—he was sitting on a lawn chair, thumbing a guitar. "But she wasn't here tonight. She said she might come, but she didn't."

"Do you know where she might be?" Kate asked.

He stared at her for a moment, then shook his head.

Alek took a piece of paper and a pen from his jacket pocket and wrote. "Listen," he said, handing the paper to the boy, "if you see her or hear from her, give us a call, will you?"

He put his hand on the small of Kate's back and led her

through the side gate, past the driveway, and into his van. It was almost five. The first light was breaking in the east. Kate rarely saw the sun come up, and she thought how strange it was, how strange and, well, wrong, that something so beautiful could take place when Audrey was missing, that the sun could still rise when her daughter may have run away from home.

"She isn't here," Kate said. "She went somewhere, she left, I just know it. But where . . ."

"The bus station," Alek said. "What about the bus station?"

"You're right, let's go."

He started the ignition, and then drove quickly, holding her hand.

They checked every seat, every nook and cranny, then went to ask the ticket seller if he'd seen her. In front of the window was a sign: "Closed 1:00 to 5:30."

"Twenty minutes," Alek said.

"Is anyone back there?" Kate peered through the metal bars and saw a woman drinking a cup of coffee, reading the newspaper. "Excuse me? I'm sorry to disturb you, but this is important."

"We're closed till five-thirty. I can't sell you a ticket till then. See the sign?"

"We don't want to buy a ticket, we want to ask you if you've seen somebody. A girl, thirteen years old, long hair, auburn, kind of—"

"I haven't gotten on yet, lady. My shift don't even start yet. I haven't seen anyone. 'Cept you."

"May we speak to whoever worked here during the night?" Alek asked.

"That'd be John Parker," the woman said. "He comes on again tonight at seven."

"Tonight at seven! We can't wait—" Kate began.

"This is an emergency," Alek told the woman. "This girl might be running away from home. Please, may we have this man's number?"

"Oh no, we can't give that out."

"Please," Kate said.

"Look, lady, I could lose my job. Besides, he works a morning job too. He wouldn't even be home."

"Do you know where he works?"

"Something about security, I think. Sorry," she added, and returned to her coffee and paper.

Kate and Alek looked at each other. "Well," Alek said.

"I'll check the bathroom," Kate told him.

"Good idea."

The bathroom was run-down in the way of bus station bathrooms at five a.m., with chipped tiles and rusty faucets and soggy toilet paper on the cracked tiled floor. Save for a single crazed fly buzzing around the closed window, it was empty, and smelled of vomit and urine and lost hope.

"1 guess we should go home now," Alek said, when they were in the van. "We should call the police."

The police. It sounded so final, so irrevocable: missing

child. Kate had an image of Audrey's face on one of those blue-and-white "Have you seen me?" ads; the rest of her life would be spent searching for her. She'd hire a detective. She and Alek would drive around town putting up flyers, and then she'd wait by the phone. She'd wait for weeks, months, years. Every time the phone rang she would jump.

Kate had thought her mom had been doing terrible, but now she understood that it was amazing, simply amazing, that she managed to wake up, get out of bed, fall asleep again, day after day, knowing she'd lost her child.

"I should have told Audrey right away," Kate said, as they turned the corner of her mother's street. "I should have told her that I was the one who kept them apart. Then this never would have happened."

Alek didn't seem to be listening. "What's that noise?" he asked.

"What noise?"

He rolled down his window with the electric button. "Listen."

It was the sound of a power tool, a lawn mower, an engine.

"Someone's mowing a lawn."

"Who would mow the lawn at five-thirty in the morning?"

"Exactly," Alek said.

Then Kate noticed the lights. It was the weekend, and early, so early that the only person on the street was the paper boy, on a black mountain bike, making his rounds, but lights were on in every house near her mom's. Porch lights, bedroom lights, lights in downstairs living rooms, a silhouette behind a sheer curtain, someone stretching long arms. A dog was barking. Somewhere close by, a baby cried. Alek pulled into the driveway and turned off the ignition, and the sound grew even louder.

They hurried out of the van and followed the noise through the wrought-iron gate, down the side of the house, and into the backyard. What Kate saw was a mirage, a refreshing blue lake in the desert: she was seeing only what she wanted to see— Audrey pushing the mower with all her might, her shoulders straining, her back hunched over, sweat glistening on her face. Kate closed her eyes, telling herself to get a grip, but when she opened them, Audrey was still there. Safe. Alive. Mowing the overgrown lawn.

Alek slid down the wall until he was crouching, balanced on the balls of his feet, apparently too relieved to stand. Audrey stopped mowing, wiped her forehead with the sleeve of her sweater, and looked over at Kate. Her expression was one of sheer, confident nonchalance, a typical teenager mowing a typical lawn on a typical weekend morning, as though she were saying, What?

Kate felt another presence, another gaze. She turned to the raised deck and saw her mother, sitting in a cushiony patio chair, wearing her fuzzy blue bathrobe and those grinning-monkey slippers on her feet, a coffee mug on the glass table by her side. She was gazing at the grass, at her granddaughter. Something was different about her, and it took Kate a few seconds to realize what it was. All the hardness had left her mother's body. Her jaw was slack, her cheeks were puffy, even her back was slouched. She looked tired, sad, like a fighter who has finally given up.

A pressure in her left palm: Alek's hand. It felt warm and comforting on top of her fingers, which were tingling with blood and oxygen and relief. The sky was becoming bluer now. Birds chirped above the lawn mower's whir. Audrey had returned to her mowing, and was struggling slowly on. Kate knew that she should go and yell at her, ask her how she could have worried them half to death, ground her into middle age, but somehow she didn't have the heart. She stood there, resting against her mother's house, holding Alek's hand, admiring the paleness of her daughter's fingers against the black rubber handles of the mower, the stretch of her reddish tangled mane above the bright green grass, watching as she performed her mysterious work. It was a beautiful sight.

Most of that day, Audrey slept. Kate checked on her twice, not so much to make sure she was there as simply to take a look at her, Paw-Paw between her chest and arms, Rosie at the foot of her bed. Around noon it began to sprinkle, and Alek—who had gone home to shower and change—came over with bagels, lox, and cream cheese, and a thousand-piece jigsaw puzzle of a southern mansion.

"It was the cheesiest one in the store. I figured if I was going to buy us a jigsaw puzzle, I might as well go whole-hog."

Kate smiled at him. "It's perfect."

They sat at the kitchen table, spread cream cheese on their

bagels and piled lox on top, and then scattered out the puzzle pieces.

"How do you want to start?" Kate asked.

"Let's sort by color. Then we'll do the borders."

Kate started sorting. Alek moved one of the pieces she had set among the pink bougainvillea into another pile.

"Hey."

"That's pink from the sky, not the flowers. See the difference?"

"You've got to be kidding. How long is this going to take us? A year?"

Alek smiled. "That depends how long it rains."

"What'll we do when it's done?"

"Anything we want. Tear it apart. Donate it to the Goodwill. Frame it and save it for posterity."

"I think we should hang it above our bed."

The word hovered in the air—had she really said "our"?— but if Alek noticed, he didn't let on.

They had finished the border when Kate's mother entered the room and sat down next to Alek.

"Mary," he said, "we could use a little help here, if you wouldn't mind."

At first she only observed, but then, as if despite herself, she began on the upper right corner, a bluish-white cloud in the sunset-pink sky.

"Someone stuck a piece of the flowers in here," she said gruffly.

"Oh, I need that piece," Kate said.

They worked mostly in silence. At two-thirty Kate heard water running upstairs, and soon after, Audrey came into the kitchen, wearing her flannel pajama bottoms and a sweatshirt, rubbing her eyes.

Nobody said a word. Audrey poured herself a glass of juice and sat down at the empty chair. She picked up a piece of the brick chimney, tried it in one spot and then another, until it fit. She studied the detail, satisfied, and selected another piece.

Without looking up from his third-floor verandah, Alek said: "I think you should know. You scared the shit out of us."

When Audrey finally opened her mouth, Kate expected something sarcastic, something that would match the defiant look on her face, something like, "You're just lucky I came back." Instead Audrey whispered, "I'm sorry."

Kate thought that was too easy. "Truly?" she asked. "Or are you just trying to avoid the guillotine?"

"I didn't mean to scare you, Mom. I'm sorry that I did."

Kate reached over and grasped Audrey's thin wrist, squeezing it, tightly, between her fingers. "Just don't do it again," Kate told her. They held each other's gaze for a long, charged moment, and then Audrey looked away, and Kate let go.

The following morning, Kate joined her mother on the deck, where she was reading the Sunday paper. She didn't look up from her article as she spoke. "It's time for you to go home," her mother said.

Kate gazed at the freshly cut grass. "Yes, I suppose you're right."

Even Rosie seemed to feel at home in their condo. Once she'd finished exploring, she found a perch on the purple velvet armchair in Audrey's room, where she looked as regal as a queen.

"Mom?" Audrey said, when Kate went into her room with a hamper of fresh laundry. "It feels good to be back home."

"It does, doesn't it?" She glanced at the papers all over Audrey's desk. When was the last time they'd discussed Audrey's homework? What on earth had she been doing in school? "What homework did you have this weekend?"

"Just geometry and Spanish."

"Did you do it?"

"Not yet."

Kate glanced at the clock on Audrey's nightstand. "*The X-Files* starts soon," she said. "You'd better get going."

It was their favorite show, the only one they never missed. Kate would make Rice Krispies treats. They'd eat them warm, unable to wait until they hardened, their fingers sticky with marshmallows as they pulled apart each sugary-sweet bite.

Kate turned around at Audrey's door. "Audrey?" she said. "Where were you going to go?"

"Nowhere. I don't know."

"We can't lie to each other anymore," Kate said quietly.

Audrey met her eyes. "What difference does it make? I came home, didn't I?"

Kate studied her for a moment, then nodded. "All right. But from now on, when we have a problem, we talk. *¿Comprende?*"

"*Comprendo*. Mom?" she added.

"Yes?"

"What's for dinner?"

Kate smiled at this quotidian question. "I thought I'd make tostadas."

"*Qué bueno.*"

Kate went into the kitchen and grated some cheese. Luke was dead. Luke was dead. Luke was dead. But the rest of them— they were alive.

As soon as Audrey left for school the following morning, Kate went into her studio. She swept the floor, washed her tools, cleaned the table, and sat down to work. She stared at the image of her own face. It was good—the face was good—and it had the potential to be something better, something more. She ran her finger over the gash on top of her skull, trying to imagine Audrey emerging. It made sense to her now—she understood perfectly what she'd been trying to do—but the idea no longer excited her. Instead of the original charge, she felt only boredom, as though she had finished that piece and moved on. Audrey was al-ready her own person, as separate from her as her mom, or Alek, or Luke. Kate had learned this the hard way.

She went to her bag of clay, scooped out a hunk, and rolled it between her palms, thinking, waiting, listening. And then she had an idea.

The days ahead had a quiet, steady rhythm. She worked in her studio, took a shower and changed in time to pick up Audrey from school. In the evenings Alek came over. Kate found herself putting on lipstick, blow-drying her hair, things she had never done before, not even when they'd first started going out. Sometimes she felt almost shy around him lately. One afternoon, when Sandira was over and the two girls were playing tennis at the condominium courts, Kate went to the mall and tried on a satiny scoop-neck shirt and a pair of low-rise velveteen jeans. Too sexy. Not at all her. She bought them anyway.

Alek took her to their favorite jazz club, made them *cioppino,* came over with an old movie, the same kinds of things he'd always done, yet it seemed to Kate that he was trying too hard to act as if he didn't notice a thing.

"What's happening with us?" Kate asked him one night.

Alek smiled. "What do you think is happening?"

"I asked you first."

"I don't know."

"Me either."

"But I hope it keeps on happening," Alek said.

He kissed her, his tongue slipping lightly into her mouth. It tasted sweet, and a tantalizing combination of exotic and familiar, like dried fruit.

A week before Thanksgiving. Audrey was mowing the lawn with the brand-new, state-of-the-art power mower Kate's mother had bought, cutting easy stripes, walking quickly, blowing bubbles with her gum. Saturday was her mowing day, not Friday. Friday would have been too loaded, too painful, and besides, Kate's mother was no longer home Friday evenings: she was working at the local soup kitchen.

"That's great," Kate had said when her mom had told her this. "Mom, that's really—"

"Don't get any ideas," her mother had said. "I'm doing it for purely selfish reasons. It makes me feel better to be around people who've had it worse than I have, that's all. And besides, they're good customers. They love my mushroom bisque."

Now Kate and her mother were watching Audrey from the patio chairs, sipping coffee.

"I've been thinking," Kate said. "About Thanksgiving?"

At this word, her mother edged forward in her seat, bracing herself.

"Thanksgiving," she repeated.

"I was thinking that maybe we should invite Sam and Colleen and the kids. What do you think?"

The skin under her mother's eyes was bloated and tender; her lips were chapped; her short gray hair needed a trim. She glanced at Kate, then turned away, as if she didn't want her daughter to see her.

"All right," she finally said.

Alek and her mother were the chefs. They'd scanned *Bon Appétit, Food & Wine,* and a half-dozen cookbooks, until they'd come up with a menu: turkey with apricot glaze, shiitake-and-hazelnut stuffing, potatoes savoyarde, sweet potato wedges with olive oil and rosemary, cranberry-and-orange relish, green beans with almonds, a carrot-and-dill puree. All Kate had to do was set the table and help chop. Audrey, who had been making cookies by herself since she was five, was in charge of dessert; she had decided on pumpkin cupcakes and gingerbread topped with vanilla whipped cream.

When Kate walked into her mom's on Thursday morning, the house already smelled like roasted turkey and thyme. Alek and her mother were in the kitchen, wearing denim aprons, and Kate admired their careful choreography, the way they moved back and forth from the cupboards to the sink to the oven and stove without getting in each other's way.

"Okay, put me to work. What can I do?" Kate said, and gave Alek a kiss. "Good morning."

"You can make us coffee," he replied. "And then you can sit down with it and relax for a while. Good morning, honey. We don't need you quite yet."

"Grandma, do you have cloves?" Audrey asked in greeting.

"Of course I have cloves."

"I told you, Mom. Is it okay if I start my gingerbread now?"

"Be my guest," Kate's mom said.

Kate ground some beans, put on a pot of coffee, and then watched her mother, her daughter, and Alek measuring flour, whipping eggs, shelling chestnuts in silent harmony: preparing their holiday feast.

"Grandma! Grandma!" Two children running into the house and then wrapping their arms around Kate's mother's waist; a huge Old English sheepdog, barking wildly, clicking its nails on the hardwood floors; a pan crashing in the kitchen, cries of "Oh, no!" and "It's all right" and "Humphrey, come back here! Stay! Sit! Jesus, Sammy, will you get the dog, I'm gonna drop this pie": Sam and Colleen had arrived.

"Well, here we are," Colleen said, and gestured toward Sam. "You remember this guy, don't you?"

Sam smiled, shaking his head. His sandy hair was fading and receding; crow's-feet were creeping in. He looked older than thirty-five, and tired, but his sparkling light brown eyes, his smile—they were exactly the same.

"Wow. Kate. It's good to see you."

"You too," she said, though it wasn't. Seeing him caused her no pain, no fear, not even a memory of a jolt of sexual attraction, just a wave of nausea that made her mouth taste sour, and then vanished. It was over. There. That wasn't so bad. Was it?

"I'm sure you're anxious to see Aud—" she began, but Audrey was already standing beside her, looking at Sam.

She was wearing a plaid felt skirt and a velour tee; her hair was down, clean and wavy—she looked lovely, and poised. She was smiling at him shyly.

"Audrey," he said. "You're even more beautiful than . . . than in your pictures." He paused, then said, "Is it all right? I mean, can I . . ." He laughed, wiped his eyes, and said, "Listen, give your old man a hug, will you?"

They hugged, Sam patting Audrey's back, Audrey looking as though she didn't know where to put her cheek, and then they broke apart.

Nobody knew what to say.

"How was your drive?" Kate said, breaking the silence.

"Don't ask," Sam replied.

Colleen shrugged. "It was a little noisy, but we managed."

"Excuse me," Audrey said. "I have to go check on my gingerbread now."

"Is that what smells so good?" Colleen gave Audrey a hug.

"Gingerbread?" Sam asked. "I love gingerbread. My mom used to make those houses. You know, with the windows out of icing, and the gumdrop roofs—"

"This isn't a house," Audrey told him. "It's just gingerbread."

"Oh. Yeah. I like that too."

Colleen and Kate exchanged glances. Kate smiled. "Let's go into the kitchen. There are a couple little people I'd like to meet."

"Just a tablespoon more," Alek was telling Kate's niece, as she added dill to the puree. "There, that's right."

"Mommy, I'm helping Mr. Alek cook."

Jennifer had hair the color of Colleen's, cut tomboy-short, and a wide-eyed expression that reminded Kate of Audrey when she was her age.

"I lost my assistant," Alek said, "so I had to get a new recruit. Colleen, good to see you." He kissed her on the cheek.

"Alek, this is Sam. Sam, Alek Perez," Kate said.

They shook hands, two men united by their love for two women who happened to be sisters—that was all.

"Hello, Mary, happy Thanksgiving," Sam said.

"Sam," she answered curtly, then went back to her cooking. Kate couldn't help smiling, though she looked down, trying to hide it. So this was how her mother acted around Sam. She visited Phoenix three or four times a year, had helped him finance his garage, invested money for his children's education, but didn't hug him, didn't kiss him, didn't even greet him with the word "hello."

"Jenny, Ryan, say hello to your aunt Kate."

Jennifer looked up, gave her a big smile, said, "Hi, Aunt Kate," and went back to the puree.

Ryan was a pint-sized version of Sam, except for the miniature wire-rimmed glasses on his nose. He extended his hand. "Nice to meet you," he said, his voice surprisingly low.

"Well, it's very nice to finally meet you."

"Mom says you're an artist. I like to draw too."

"Do you? Maybe we can draw later on."

He smiled. "Okay."

Kate's mother surveyed the kitchen, glanced at Alek, and said, "Well? I think we're just about ready."

It was time to say grace. Her mother had done this every year—it was her job, her role, just as carving the turkey had been Luke's—but she stood with a perplexed expression on her face. Kate wondered if she'd forgotten how to pray.

"Can I say grace, please?" Jennifer asked.

"No," Colleen said. "Of course not, your grandmother will—"

"Go ahead," Kate's mother said. "Jennifer, you go right ahead."

Jennifer recited a standard Catholic-school prayer. When she had finished, Kate said, "Let's dig in," and began to pass around the platters. Alek carved the turkey and took orders for white and dark meat.

The conversation began generally, and broke into groups. Sam, seated next to Audrey, asked her what her favorite subjects were, what sports she played, what kind of music she liked, standard adult-to-teenager questions. When everyone had finished eating, the room suddenly became silent.

Colleen smiled. "An angel passed by."

"Maybe it's Uncle Luke," Ryan offered.

"It's amazing, isn't it?" Kate said. "That it took Luke's death to bring us together like this."

Her mother looked pained, but there was a softness to her expression that made Kate think that she didn't mind hearing this, that perhaps she had been thinking the same thing.

"To Luke," Alek said quietly, raising his wineglass. "To his life, and to his being at peace."

"To Luke."

"To Uncle Luke."

A few seconds passed, like a transcontinental pause, before their mother whispered, "To Luke."

After dinner, everyone scattered. Audrey and Jennifer played horse at the basketball hoop Alek had attached to the garage, while Ryan drew with pastels at the kitchen table, and Sam went into the family room to watch football on TV. After a wink from Alek that let Kate know he knew football was a violent barbaric sport but didn't want to be rude, he said, "I think I'll join you,

Sam," and followed him into the family room. Kate and Colleen put things away, and then, over the sound of the dishwasher, Colleen said, "I hope I can see your place before we go back home."

"Why not now?"

"Really?"

"Yeah, we can take a ride over, and I can feed the cat while we're there."

"I'd like that."

Kate went to tell Alek she was leaving. She stood directly in front of the television set. "Listen, Colleen and—"

"Kate, get out of the way!"

"What happened?"

"I don't know, did he intercept?"

Wild cheers came from the television; Kate stood behind Alek and kissed him on top of the head. "I'll be back in an hour," she said.

"Yeah, honey, all right."

"Here's the replay," Sam said.

Kate returned to the kitchen. "Sammy won't even know I'm gone," Colleen said. "He's got his game, his beer, someone to watch it with. Ryan, if Humphrey barks, you let him in, because your father won't notice a thing."

"Okay, Mom." Ryan didn't even look up from his drawing.

"Let's get out of here," Colleen said.

Kate smiled. "I'm just gonna go tell Mom."

When she got to the top of the landing, she heard a faint noise, a cross between a whisper and a wail. She approached her mother's door, which was open a few inches. Her mother was sitting on the edge of the bed, her face in profile, her body rocking gently back and forth. Tears streamed down her cheeks. Kate wanted to go and hug her, say something comforting, but she knew she had to let her be. The sounds coming from her were stifled, choked, yet those tears—they ran out of her eyes, down her cheeks, rivers of grief spilling all at once.

Kate had given Colleen a tour of the living room, dining room, kitchen, and baths, and now they were in her bedroom. Colleen was pointing to a picture of Alek, holding up a trout, taken on their first camping trip.

"He's very cute," she said.

"Do you think so?" Kate replied, and the sharpness in her voice surprised her.

"Kate, you don't think . . . I mean, I would never. Never. I'd rather die first. You know that, don't you?"

Kate nodded. "Yeah, I think I do."

Colleen smiled, set the picture down. "Besides, any idiot can see that he's totally in love with you. He probably hasn't even looked at another wom—"

"And Sam wasn't?"

Colleen shook her head. "No, Kate. I don't think he was."

"I know. I know he wasn't. But you know what? I don't think I was that in love with him, either. I mean, I was. I thought I was. But when I found out about your affair, underneath the rage and the humiliation and all those other things, I felt something like relief. I mean, let's face it, we really didn't have anything in common, we probably would have gotten divorced eventually anyway. This way, I could be the victim. It was so easy."

Kate had barely admitted these thoughts to herself, but now, as she spoke them aloud to her sister, they felt true.

"God. That seems like so long ago. Does it seem so long ago to you?"

"A lifetime."

"You know, I always wanted to write you a letter or something, try to explain myself, or at least tell you how sorry I was."

"Why didn't you?"

"It didn't seem like the kind of thing you could apologize for. But I was. Am. Sorry, I mean."

She looked penitent but impatient—they might have been talking about a sweater Colleen had borrowed without permission, and then ruined—and for a moment, Kate experienced the full force of that old rage. It was like falling into an abyss. Nothing mattered: you could eat or starve, live or die. Your self dissolved into a nothingness that wasn't nirvana but the painful burning of a soul in hell, and the only way out was your hatred for the people who had sent you there, combined with your love for your child.

Colleen pouted, waiting for Kate to say something, but Kate wasn't quite ready to give in. She studied her sister's face. She was searching for Luke, in her mouth, in her blue eyes. Colleen: her only living sibling.

"Hey," Kate said. "There's something I want you to see."

Kate's neck, glazed a porcelain white, rested on the table in her studio; her face, now glazed in colors—mouth reddish-brown, eyes green, eyebrows the coppery red of her hair—stared out above her neck; atop her skull, nestled in a crown of thorns, nine figures protruded from her head. Audrey refused to be the one-sided object of anyone's gaze, and stared back into the viewer's eyes. Alek was beside Audrey, pointing upward, identifying some constellation that only he could see. Kate's mother's face was creviced by wrinkles—she was old, as old as the hills, as the earth, old as time—her skin glazed a primeval reddish brown, her back straight, erect, strong. Colleen looked both innocent and sexy, a carnal angel in an old print dress. Sam stood beside her, facing her, his body in profile, carrying a wrench in one hand and his own bloody heart in the other. Ryan and Jennifer were on their hands and knees, their heads bent close together, one of them (it didn't matter which—they were beige, generic, two kids) whispering a secret in the other's ear. Next to them, beside his grandchildren, the grandchildren he'd never met, was Kate and Colleen and Luke's father, wearing boots, his hands disproportionately large, like God's hands, a pair of ethereal wings jutting out of his back. And then there was Luke. He was wearing glasses; his hair was disheveled; the long fingers of one hand stroked his chin. His head was cocked slightly to the side, as though he was trying to figure something out, or perhaps he was just listening to something, sad music playing softly in the background.

They were inside Kate, and outside. They were their own selves, but because she couldn't know these own selves, they were also whom she imagined them to be. They were her crown of thorns, her halo of flowers. They were her family. The people she'd loved and hated. The people who'd helped her become who she was. They were her angels, her demons, her ghosts.

Colleen stretched out her index finger and touched Luke's tiny lips. "It's funny," she said, "but right now, seeing him here, I don't miss him as much. It's like he's really here."

"I call it *Self-Portrait with Ghosts*," Kate said.

"Ghosts?"

"Nobody's who they used to be." Kate looked at her sister and smiled. "Least of all me."

It was dark when they went back to their mother's. Everyone was inside, even the enormous dog, who lay under the kitchen table, gnawing on a bone. The room smelled delicious, of ginger and cinnamon and cloves. With the postgame on TV as background, Sam talked Alek's ear off about cars: "No, those are good, they run a long time, the only thing you have to watch on them is the clutch." Their mother was making coffee, while the kids whipped cream for the gingerbread.

"Can you swim in the ocean in the winter?" Ryan was asking Audrey.

"No, the water's too cold. But we can go there for a walk."